Adam and Belle

Gabriella Bartula

Adam and Belle

Copyright © 2018 by Gabriella Bartula. All rights reserved.

No part of this reproduction may be reproduced, stored in a retrieval system or transmitted in any way by any means, electronic, mechanical, photocopy, recording or otherwise without prior permission of the author except as provided by the USA copyright law.

Dedicated to my family and friends.
Thank you for all the encouragement!

You have all heard the story of a French damsel and a magically mutated prince. The story is one of love and happy feelings, holding within the pages a very good moral: do not judge one by their outward appearance. Brace yourselves, you have been told a **lie!**

That is right, a lie! A false tale! An incorrect account! I know you are probably shocked, some of you are maybe even crying. Do not despair; there is hope, for I have placed the burden of truth upon my shoulders. Now, the story I am about to recount will not be the same, but at least my tale will be the truth.

So, make the choice. Do you choose to conform and be like others who will shut this book and continue believing the lie, or are you going to be one of the elite who are bold and courageous, and yearn for the correct story? But beware. Once you start on this adventure, you can never turn back, and you will never be the same.

I knew I could count on you. Let us begin.

Chapter One

A Boy Alone

"Prince Adam!"

The young prince grinned smugly when he heard the maid screeching from behind his bedroom's door. Adam knew the girl, Estelle, was frustrated; he supposed she had the right to be. The prince had played some harmless tricks on the servants earlier in the day, and that always ruffled Estelle, who had become the prince's self-appointed guardian. Though Adam's parents never gave their verbal agreement, the prince knew they secretly loved having someone else watching their child.

As the maid began rapping her fist on the door, Adam assumed he should at least give the poor woman an answer. He smiled and took pleasure in how easily he could perturb Estelle. "Go away," came the chilled reply. "I wish not to see a single soul until my parents return!" The prince stifled a laugh as he imagined the shock and anger raging across the maid's face. The answer was perhaps a little too dramatic, but there was no taking it back now. At this pace, he would have her as ruffled as her feather duster by the end of the conversation.

"*Mon Cher*," the maid said coaxingly, "Dinner has been prepared in honor of your special day. I was sent to bring you down. Imagine how foolish you would make me look if I was to go back without you by my side! I am sure a boy as *sweet* as you would not do that to his friend. Please, come out."

Adam began to feel angry himself; he could tolerate a maid who was overly concerned about his attitude and upbringing, but he was furious that Estelle was patronizing him and talking to him like he was a little child. In his anger, the prince felt vindicated to say whatever he wanted. "I know of your crafty ways, Estelle. Jean Claude and you have probably concocted some sort of revenge to repay for my earlier pranks. That is all they were: harmless pranks to amuse me in my time of boredom. I do not wish to sit and eat amongst hypocrites and two-faces who wish my demise."

Estelle started to snap at the prince but remembered her place. She turned and haughtily skulked down the hallway. She let the harsh *click-clack* of her heeled shoes audibly voice her frustration.

Meanwhile, Adam paced about his room, tossing an uneaten apple between his hands. He stared at a picture of his absent parents, the monarchs of France. The picture was old and slightly worn around the edges, but otherwise it was perfectly preserved. In the picture, the king and queen cradled baby Adam in their arms and smiled ever so pleasantly. Those were cherished, but almost forgotten times.

Now Adam was too grown up to be held in his parents' arms. This was his thirteenth birthday. He was a young man who needed to be helped by no one but himself. His parents obviously agreed with this philosophy, for they often left Adam alone; they had done so this very night. "Royal business," the king curtly replied as the queen and he hurried out of the castle, leaving their son to fend for himself once again.

Adam had grown to accept that he would just have the type of parents that never stayed at home, and he was fine with that. But why did he feel so uncomfortable about his father's absence? Did he miss them? Yes, and he also loved them, but love had never made him feel this way before. Maybe his parents' peculiar attitude was the perplexing factor in this situation.

King Avery had begun to receive strange letters half a fortnight ago. Neither the letters nor the mysterious couriers who delivered them bothered the prince, but the king's noticeable change in conduct and countenance worried him terribly. Adam thought his father was the bravest man alive, one who could be threatened by nothing, yet these letters seemed to shake him terribly. King Avery, once the mighty oak of France, had been reduced to a quaking aspen by a piece of parchment.

The queen's endless crying did not help Adam either. Three days before the mysterious departure, the young prince found his mother in a frenzied state in the East Wing. She had thrown herself upon her bed and sobbed uncontrollably. In her right hand she grasped one of the cursed epistles, which had now been reduced to a crumpled, tear-stained mess. Adam's blood boiled with rage at the fact that someone had been able to tear the once-happy family asunder. He wished to comfort his mother, but thought his silence wise. Adam retreated from the room and left his mother alone in her time of lamenting.

Adam wished he could decipher his parents' odd behavior. To be able to know what troubled their souls would begin to ease his own. Adam was currently considering asking the servants what they knew of the situation, but immediately dismissed the idea. The prince mocked his own stupidity. *"To stoop so low as to ask for help. Adam, what were you thinking? However, I do want to know what is going on. Oh how I wish I knew!"*

Sixteen Years Prior

King Aso sat upon his once-glorious throne. The neighboring willows waved their outstretched branches toward the distraught king, and the towering oaks groaned, echoing the cries of the king's heart. The previously tranquil waters rippled violently, moved by the king's aura of anger. The fairy's broken soul cast an air of abandonment upon his smooth face and his wings sagged. They, which were at one time filled with vitality and joy, were now weighed down by the weight of depression.

    Jezé (the king's second wife) stood in the shadows of the courtroom. From her fortress of airy darkness, she glowered at her husband. She bit her tongue, holding back the rage and contempt that boiled from deep within her. King Aso was no longer a dream in her eyes, but a curse. He had become a foolish man whose brains were decaying inside his old head. Jezé took a few relaxing breaths to calm her disturbed nerves. Then, with grace and elegance, she strolled toward the king, her thin, black wings trailing behind her like a mourner's veil.

    Jezé sidled up to her husband. "My dear Aso," her voice deceptively sweet, "Fret no more over your traitorous son. Please turn your attention towards your failing kingdom . . . and to me." She leaned in and gave her husband an alluring kiss. As she drew out of her vampish bite, she expected to be greeted by her husband's attentive eyes, yet King Aso looked beyond Jezé instead, his dulled eyes searching for his son.

Jezé growled in frustration and pushed herself off the throne, upset she could no longer manipulate her husband with arousing flirtations.

The king's son, by his first marriage, was a headstrong lad named Avanari. The prince had shunned his kingdom and birthright, throwing them away recklessly in hopes of winning a young maiden's hand in marriage. The fairy prince's heart, stolen so easily by a human girl, often wandered from home. Although fairy law did not allow human marriage, Avanari chased after the girl passionately, and no one could convince Avanari that he was being foolish. "This girl loves me as I am, and if I am being foolish in returning her love, then it is a madness I will embrace," replied the prince when questioned about his actions.

Fairy law also required that the reigning king or queen execute anyone who disobeyed. However, King Aso could not bring himself to kill his son, so he simply banished him. Jezé saw Avanari as a weakness of her husband. *"If my husband is to conquer the world for me, he cannot. Be. Weak!"* The dark queen decided to take matters into her own hands. "Enno! Anno!" Jezé summoned her two assassins with a sharp, cutting tone. The two servants came and bowed before their queen.

"What does-s-s-s our queen reques-s-s-st of us-s-s-s? As-s-s-sk us-s-s-s our queen and your wis-s-s-sh is-s-s-s…"

Jezé's hands dashed out at viper speed. She clasped Enno's scrawny neck and Anno's fatty arm, and her stiletto nails dug into their scaly flesh. Her face, which was considered perfectly beautiful by most, curled up into a hateful sneer as she spoke. "Now listen, you fools! I have an important job for you," her voice was low and hissing, "If you breathe a word about this to anyone they will be the last words you speak. Now here is what I need you to do." Her voice flowed on as she recounted her malicious plan to her slaves. A sly and devious look crossed Enno's face, and Anno rubbed his hands together, greedy for blood. "Cons-s-s-sider the tas-s-s-sk completed, your highness-s-s-s," the two fairies replied in unison.

Chapter Two

A Brave Attempt

"*Awaaake, young prince, and saaave your paaarents! Awaaake!*"

The willows and birches scrapped their spindly fingers across the castle's panes. They felt disturbance in every breeze that rustled through their leaves. Something was desperately wrong, and they knew that they must warn the prince. "*Awaaake young prince!*"

"FATHER!"

Adam awoke in the dead of night, his arm outstretched to a parent who was not there. His satin nightgown was saturated in sweat and his pillow smothered in tears. His short, chestnut-blond curls clung desperately to his flushed and sticky face. Adam had spent the last three hours tossing his way through a horrible dream, feeling as though he would have been forever trapped in that nightly vision if an invisible force had not pulled him out. Adam did not know where to go, but he knew that his parents' lives depended on him taking action. The prince was quickly up and dressed in his best traveling clothes, his satchel slung around his shoulder, carrying only the necessities.

Adam was in such a crazed state that he did not consider his steps. As he arrived at the first rung of descending stairs, the troubled boy did not slow down his frenzied pace. Adam tumbled and slid down the thirty steps, bumping his head and appendages multiple times. As he reached the bottom of the stairs, Adam was out of breath. Thankfully, the prince had not broken a bone in his body, but his pride quickly took a beating when he looked up and saw a chubby face staring back at him; the young boy had seen the whole ordeal.

"Why you fall down, Pwince Adam?"

The prince slowly stood up and dusted himself off. "No reason, Chip. I was just in a hurry and wasn't looking where I placed my feet."

Timothy, son of Mrs. Agatha Kettlery, was the only one in the entire castle that Adam considered his friend and confidant. The petite, charismatic boy was half Adam's age, but the prince loved him anyways. He had earned the nickname "Chip" from the characteristic gap between his front two teeth; his smile was something that could always brighten Adam's day.

"Why was you in a hu–wee, Adam? You gonna go somepwace?"

Adam suddenly began to regret his rash decision. If this was the type of venture from whence few returned, Adam would have a difficult time saying goodbye to his friend. However, he could not let his parents face certain doom alone. He would never forgive himself if his parents died and he had intentionally forfeited the ability to stop their terrible fate.

The young prince knelt down in front of Timothy. "Chip ol' boy," Adam began, tousling his friend's soft hair, "Remember the story you love so much, the one of the gallant knight who left everything behind so that he could rescue someone he loved? Well, I am to live out that story this very night. I believe my parents are in grave danger, and I must be the one to save them. Do you understand?"

Poor Timothy was nearly in tears. "You gonna weave me, Pwince Adam? Momma say your pay–wents ah alwight. Do . . . Do you hafta go?" Little droplets started to roll down the lad's flushed cheeks.

"Yes, Timothy. But we must keep a firm upper lip and be brave. I will be back soon. I will make a deal with you. When I get back, *if* I hear a good report on how brave you were in my absence, you can have all my horse figurines."

That lifted the boy's countenance immediately. With a grin as large as the moon, Timothy Kettlery ran off down the hall, giddily shouting, "Ho–ses, ho–ses, I get ho–ses!" As Adam turned to exit the castle, he sighed within himself, hoping he could return to fulfill his promise.

A dark and daunting forest has the potential to spook anyone, especially when one is alone. As Adam gallantly rode through the Barrier Forest on horseback, he tried to ignore the ghostly trees and indistinct noises. He placed his hand on the hilt of his sword, taking comfort in the memory of his long lessons in fencing. "If any villain should come upon me in the night, I shall be ready."

His horse, Antoinette, did not seem to believe her master's daring words, for she fearfully nickered and shook her darkened mane. The prince leaned forward and smoothed the bristled hair on Antoinette's neck, soothingly reassuring his horse's safety. However, Antoinette still seemed to be panicked, for at the first questionable noise, she bolted.

Outstretched tree limbs, prickly briars, and dangling vines scratched and entangled Adam's body as he rode haphazardly through the forest. "Antoinette! Whoa girl, slow down!" Adam pulled so hard on the leather reigns that they violently snapped in half; the ends lashed back and cut into the prince's flesh, marring his left cheek. Antoinette, finally exhausted from the midnight gallop, slowed to a steady walk. Adam, a cloth pressed firmly against his cheek, surveyed the surrounding area. "My effort to look at a map would be pointless. A good night's rest will clear my head."

Up ahead, the young prince saw a circular clearing, a perfect place to start a fire and sleep under the stars. As soon as Adam reached the perimeter of the clearing, his body froze and his heart was clutched by fear. A howl or two echoed in nearby bushes. "*Wolves!*" Struggling with all his might to be silent, Adam was able to turn around and start walking in the opposite direction. He stopped when he heard voices. "Mother? Fa-father?" He almost leapt for joy at the recognition of his parent's blessed voices. He turned around once more and ran towards his parents.

But he was stopped, for as soon his legs began to move, Adam was pushed down to the ground. The briars threatened to poke his eyes, and the soft ground clung to his bloody cheek. Two paws were firmly pressed into the prince's back, and sticky drool oozed onto the nape of Adam's neck. The wolves howled again, this time sounding much closer. Straining, Adam lifted his head just enough to see a horrendous sight. Tears began to streak his face.

No more than five yards in front of him, the king and queen stood, surrounded by a pack of wolves. King Avery shielded the queen with his arm while he jabbed at the wolves with his sword. The queen stood bravely beside her husband. She was ready to fight their attackers, though she was armed with nothing more than a heavy cooking pot. Despite their fearful surroundings they stood together, ready to fight and possibly die by each other's side. Love was strong even in the face of death.

Two of the wolves, the biggest and darkest, slowly rose onto their hind legs and miraculously transformed. Scaly flesh replaced matted fur, dirty fingers took the place of sharp claws, and dingy wings unfurled from their backs. Adam gasped in shock and awe. "Fairies," the prince whispered hoarsely.

I cannot transcribe the following conversation between the fairies, for they spoke in their own native tongue. The only important thing you need to know is that, yes, they are Enno and Anno. They had faithfully attended to Queen Jezé's command for sixteen years (the mission would have perhaps ended sooner if the assassins were not as dull as a butter knife). They mercilessly tracked down Prince Avanari. When they found him, they wrote blackmail letters, threatening to expose the king's heritage if he and the queen did not meet with them.

Enno and Anno told the king that the people of France would be less than pleased to find out that a dishonored fairy prince was now their ruler; they assured the king that, if he was to meet them and pay a small price, his secret would be safe. Unfortunately, the "small price" that the fairies requested was the lives of the king and queen.

Oh, that is right, I forgot to tell you! Yes, King Avery is the once headstrong, lovesick Prince Avanari. He changed his name when he married the human maiden, Princess Marie. Avery also lost all his fairy qualities when he was banished. He gave up everything: wings, powers, and heritage. The only thing he did not lose was his love for Marie.

Unfortunately, Enno and Anno were dutifully obedient and did away with the king and queen, all to Adam's horror. I dare not describe the merciless killing, for death by wolves is far too gory for a book like this. I shall summarize by saying the deaths were truly horrendous, leaving Adam emotionally scarred for a very long time.

Chapter Three

Consequences

Chilled rain fell softly on the palace grounds. Summer was dead, autumn was aging quickly, and a dreadfully gloomy winter was being born. Adam, now a buff lad of fifteen and reigning monarch of France, was sitting in the West Wing. He looked out over the gray and barren land in a critiquing way. His face seemed to reflect the weather's coldness. Over the past two years, he changed from a mischievous boy to a bitter tyrant. He did not care if he frightened everyone in the castle; his harsh behavior was just his way of venting his pain.

Adam's heart ached when he thought about how he had pushed Chip away from him. He tried to reach out to his friend, but their conversations always ended with Adam becoming enraged. As he thought about his now-dreary life, Adam sank into his high-back chair and looked around the room. He had everything: servants, money, power, and the ability to say one word and everyone obeyed his biding. "Then why do I feel so empty?" Ever since his parents' death, Adam felt emotionless and numb.

"Sire?"

"Yes, General Vicenti? Have you pleasing news for your king?"

A tall young man stood in the doorway. Afraid to come near his commanding prince (he would not think of him as his king), Vicenti did not enter the room. Even though Vicenti was only twenty-years-old, he knew that Prince Adam was not running his kingdom well. But still, a reigning monarch deserves respect, and Vicenti had to choose to respect Adam. "Yes, my king. The enemy kingdom has been found."

A fiery boldness sparked into Adam's deep brown eyes. "The enemy. *My* enemy. Found." Adam momentarily reveled in morbid satisfaction. Clearing his throat, he barked, "Assemble the men. We march now."

"But, your highness, the men. I mean, sir, dawn has not even arrived." Vicenti's stomach churned as he thought of how angry the soldiers would be when they were awoken this early.

Adam, a very persistent leader, soon forcibly convinced his general to prepare the men for battle. Soon, seventy-five men were marching on foot and horse across the French terrain. Hooves sloshed through mud and leather-clad soles stealthily maneuvered through tall grasses. Adam led his men, still on the back of faithful Antoinette, but stopped them short when they came upon a peaceful river. Adam raised his hand

and slowly lowered his fist to the ground, signaling his men to be quite and stealthy. Vicenti slinked up to his commander pointing to a clearing in the dense forest.

"Right over there, sir. That is the fairy homeland. We are sure this is where the assassins live. Our spies have informed us that they are under the direct employment of the fairy queen, Queen Jezé. So our objective, if I am not mistaken, is to capture the queen and kill her minions?"

"No. Kill the entire race. Why risk another assassin being born? I do not want to hear or see any captives, General, only corpses. Let our swords and the ground on which we stand be stained red with the blood of our victims! Let the air be fouled with the rank aroma of burning flesh."

Screams. Fire. Blood. Murder. Horses. Men. Swords. Fire. Destruction. Screams. Blood. Murder. Rage. Revenge. Fire. Blood.

Death!

A young fairy maiden, Sabella Rose, ran along the bumpy stone streets of her woodland home. The heavy soot that hung in the air blackened her cloth dress. Sabella's blush red wings drooped pitifully on the ground, becoming a tripping hazard for the frightened girl. Her feet ached and her head hurt. She wanted to stop, fall down, and embrace the deadly fate that was consuming everything around her, but she held onto the need for survival that drove her forward.

Men, *human* men from an unknown location, had come and were ransacking the town. Pyres burned everywhere and, from all directions, screams could be heard. Smoke could be smelt as it filled the air ominously. Her mother had woken Sabella Rose from ambrosial sleep; now they were running for their lives.

As Sabella ran, she recognized the bloody bodies of companions tossed on the sides of the road. Some were dead and the rest were dying, crying for mercy and help. Women wept over the bodies of their fallen husbands, their own tears cut short by a blade through the back. Children wandered around, lost and frightened, but they were put to an end no sooner than they cried out for their parents.

The loss in population was already enough to cripple any civilization, but the men still ran around, killing everyone and everything. They took no prisoners, only spoil and treasure from their victims' houses. There was one man that did not kill; he slaughtered. At first, he stayed on his horse and commanded his men, but then he became overcome with the need for blood himself. Sabella was about to dwell on her hatred for the man, but something distracted her.

"Mama, your wings!"

Enchantress, mother of Sabella Rose, turned to look at her once-beautiful wings. Somehow the lacy membrane had become a resting place for a few wandering embers that were turning the wings into black ash. "Never mind, Sabella. Just keep running!"

The cobblestone pathways soon became dirt as Enchantress and her daughter ran into the woods. Sabella Rose's feet became very heavy, and she continued to stumble over her sagging wings. Her copper hair, caked in dust, veiled her face. Soot landed upon her rich eyelashes and burrowed into her eyes, agitating them greatly. For being only thirteen summers old, Sabella had carried herself wonderfully; now her legs would not continue. "Mama, I can't . . . I can't do this anymore."

The fairy cradled her daughter, while frantically looking for a safe dwelling. Thirty yards away there was a small hole, covered mostly by large boulders, which was a perfect place to stash a treasured item. "There," Enchantress pointed, "Can you make that far, my dear?" Sabella Rose feebly nodded her head. Halfway there, the twosome heard the oncoming trampling of hooves. They could hear only one horse, but the rider's deranged cries of war alerted them to the danger that was approaching quickly.

They reached the hole, and Sabella climbed down. "Mama, this is an awfully small hole. Can you fit?"

Tears illuminated Enchantress' eyes. "No, my dear. This is the last night for the fairy race to live. I am more than willing to die, so that you might survive. But you cannot go through life as a fairy, or you will surely be killed. I hereby bind your distinguishing traits and powers, only to be unlocked when our pursuing enemy sincerely changes his heart." With that, she kissed her daughter's sooty forehead one last time and rushed off to meet her attacker. As Sabella Rose viewed her mother's retreating frame, she felt herself fall into a much yearned for sleep.

Adam drove Antoinette like mad, steering her onward, barely avoiding the trees. He had seen two fairies dash into the forest, and he pursued for the kill. He saw a green-cloaked figure up ahead. "Hyah! Faster, noble mare." Adam planned to trample the lady down, but as he neared, Antoinette stopped. The fairy's outstretched hand seemed to take control over the horse. Antoinette reared and her master fell to the ground, incredibly vexed. Adam leapt up and drew his sword, wobbling slightly from the fall like a drunken man.

"Consider your actions, boy. Once you commit a crime, you cannot undo your actions. I, Enchantress, have seen the results your actions will cause. Let me be, and I shall grant you peace."

"Peace?! I haven't seen one drop of peace since my parents... Why should I let you live?"

"I can be of much help to you and your kingdom."

"I don't need help from a peasant, especially a *fairy* peasant."

"You judge me by my sooty rags? *You* are responsible for the smoke and ash that so rests on these clothes! Oh, Adam, your heart is as cold as stone. Are you pleased living a life filled with hate? Is that something your parents would have wanted?"

"Enough. Do not mention my parents again!" The young prince tightened his grasp on the hilt of his sword.

"Why? Because the memories you have of your parents hold the last ounce of love in your heart? A love that your hate wishes to crush?" Enchantress' arms became very animated as she talked, gesturing and flailing her arms at invisible things.

"Enough."

"Get rid of this darkness in your heart, Prince Adam! Regain the love your parents showed you. Be human again, instead of this beastly monster you've become!" Enchantress drew closer to the prince, her arms outstretched like a mother yearning to draw her wayward son close.

"I said **enough!**" With speed and fury, Adam thrust his sword into Enchantress' abdomen, ripping through dress and skin. Murky blood poured from the fairy's fatal wound. Enchantress crumpled to the ground, gasping for air. She feebly raised her hand and grasped the hem of Adam's garment, pulling the prince down to her level. After placing a tiny package in his breast pocket, Enchantress looked straight into the boy's eyes and saw an inner reflection of confusion, anger, and fear. She smiled, feeling overcome by pity for the boy and peace about what was going to happen. Taking a shaky breath, Enchantress breathed out her final prophecy.

"Your hatful heart, now . . . reflected on your castle's walls . . . everyone will see . . . until you have made right the wrong, into a Beast you shall forever be."

Crumpling back down onto the ground, Enchantress tilted her head back towards the hole where she had laid down her secret treasure. With her vision starting to fade, the fairy whispered, "I love you," to her baby one last time. She tried to turn her head back to Adam, but found that her muscles were already starting to freeze and contract. At least she would die staring at where her daughter lay invisibly, rather than gazing upon her monstrous destructor. Smiling again, Enchantress breathed out for her last time.

Adam stood still as he watched the life drain out of the fairy. He felt little guilt or remorse over her; he was a warrior and ridding the world of his enemies was part of the job. However, as Adam recalled the woman's last words his eyes widened with fear. He had been cursed!

Chapter Four

A New Family

"Young lady, are you alright?"

Blurry pictures. Muffled sounds. Numb sensations. Overwhelming dizziness.

"Where are your parents?"

Splitting headache. Foggy memories. **Searing** pain between shoulder blades.

"You seem to be unconscious. Now, I am going to gently lift you out and take you into town. Monsieur Cartier should be able to help you."

Sabella felt weightless as she floated to the surface. A man held her tight. His callused hands firmly gripped her soft, limp shoulders and legs. Her head rolled around in his arms, flopping back and forth constantly. Her world did not seem right. She felt pain, she recognized her senses were disturbed, but she could not think enough to communicate. The throbbing pain that dwelt in her upper back was the worst. With every step the man took across the forest terrain, a new sting would zip up her spine, causing complete discomfort.

She looked at the man. She tried to study his face. His eyes were bright, although concerned. His thinning hair rested upon his head like a silvery halo. *"This man must be my guardian angel."* His lips moved in a rhythmic pattern; Sabella knew he was speaking, but her ears only picked up limited amounts. "Must have fallen . . . where . . . parents . . . Are they . . . alive?"

A spooky feeling overcame Sabella Rose. She knew the words the man spoke, but her brain would not allow her to put them in a comprehensive sentence. She could not, if you will, fill in the blanks. Her head turned away and rolled around some more. When she looked at the man again, his brow was deeply furrowed. Sabella, numb as her mind was, could comprehend this man's unpleasant thoughts.

"Here ya go, girl. This here is Philippe. He'll be the one to take us into town." Sabella's eyes focused on a large mass that approached them. A horse! Philippe raised his head at the sound of his master's approaching footsteps. He whinnied and craned his neck to see the mysterious bundle. Sabella felt the man's arms reposition her, sitting her upon Philippe's back. "Slowly, Philippe. Mademoiselle is rather sickly. Take us to town."

The slow ride from the forest gave Sabella a wonderful time to clear her head. Philippe's slow trot seemed to echo the rhythmic beat of her own heart. The strong, fresh smell of evergreen trees cleared her senses. The entire world seemed to be . . . peaceful. Words started to finally fit together cohesively in her head; sentences formed fluently on her tongue. Sabella straightened up and turned to face her rescuer. "Thank you, kind sir, for pulling me out of a dire circumstance."

The man jerked on his horse's reigns. He looked perplexed and confused, surprised that the girl could even speak! He cleared his throat before letting out a shaky, but enthusiastic, "You are welcome, mademoiselle." They rode on in silence for quite some time before the man's curiosity broke through. "What can you tell me about yourself?"

"My name is Sabella Rose, but my friends call me Bella or Belle, though I prefer the later. I am thirteen years old and ... and ... I don't remember anything else!" Sabella began to cry, gasp, and moan. Salty tears dampened her soft, brown eyes. "Monsieur, I ... I cannot think of anything! All I know is my name. I remember not my place of birth or who birthed me. I do remember you, however," Sabella gasped slightly and an innocent smile spread across her face as she asked, "Are you my father?"

The gentleman, Seymour Dubois by name, was torn by his current situation. Poor Belle, her parents probably dead, thought he was her father. If he told her yes, Belle would be very happy, but he did not believe lying was right. If he told her no, he would crush the already distraught girl's spirit, and he could not ever imagine doing that. He inhaled a long deep breath and slowly blew out, thinking of the commitment he was about to make.

"Yes, my dear Belle," Seymour spoke slowly, "You are correct."

Belle nearly frightened Philippe as she let out a shout of exuberant joy. "I knew I was right! You have the kind and caring face a father should have! Are we going home now, Papa?"

"Yes, yes we are going home."

Seymour was grateful for the following moment of silence. The girl asked a lot of questions and he had not had the time to completely grasp his current situation. He would have to make up a story to explain why his wife (who would be Belle's supposed mother) was dead and why he had another girl, who would now become Belle's sister. His task was slightly easier than he expected, however, because Belle had no past memory. Anything he told her, she would readily accept as the truth.

"Oh, Papa, listen! I can hear the water fairies singing and dancing! Is that not a beautiful melody? Their rhythmic steps are so graceful and breathtaking!"

Seymour once again pulled Philippe to a halt. He strained his ears to hear any faint sound of singing. Alas, the only music that touched his ears was the sound of the rushing brook. He chuckled at the idea of living fairies and at his new daughter's creative imagination. He shook his head and prodded Philippe forward. "Belle, what you hear is the stream over to our left. But I must congratulate your effort on using your keen imagination."

Belle's lips pursed together in frustration and she crossed her arms stubbornly. She looked hurt, angry, and confused. "I made nothing up, Papa. I know I heard fairies. Mother always told me they were real, surely you remember that? I am sure if I went over there, I would see what I heard: beautiful water fairies singing and dancing!" Without further notice, Belle leaped gracefully of the horse and ran in the direction of her fairies.

Seymour was left to ponder for a few moments. The girl had mentioned her mother, but the fairy-believing mademoiselle could not have been referring to his deceased wife. Seymour wondered why the girl would make up such strange tales. Perhaps she did hear fairies. Or maybe the fanciful stories were just her way of coping with the forgotten death of her real parents. The Frenchman tied up his horse and went after the distraught girl.

When Seymour finally caught up with Belle, he found her kneeling by the waters' edge. No fairies. No music or dancing. He only saw a little girl whose pretend friends did not exist. "Come Belle, we must go home now."

The girl's head whipped around, revealing a heartbroken face streaked with tears. She tried to hide her quivering lip and furrowed brows as she buried her face in her hands and moaned loudly. Seymour ran to Belle and dropped to his knees beside her. "Dearest Belle, I tried to warn you that there were nor fairies he– . . ."

"But there were fairies! Look! Look at what I have found. They have been hurt very cruelly!" Belle opened and lifted her hands to show her father what lay in her palms. A piece of torn membrane, thin and lace–like, rested in the gentle hands of Belle. Although the edges were singed, one could still make out the intricate design. "It is a piece of fairy wing. Someone must have tried to kill the poor creature for the beautiful wings!" Belle then broke into more sobs and wails, her shoulders shaking as she buried herself in Seymour's chest.

Seymour was perplexed as ever before. He cradled the weeping girl and tried to comfort her by stroking her hair and whispering encouraging phrases. When he first brushed his callused hands down her head, Seymour was shocked to find that the girl, despite spending the night in a hole, had beautiful, silky hair. As her sobs died down, Seymour suggested that the two of them should probably go home. Belle agreed and they both made their way back for Philippe.

A little less than half an hour later, Belle and Seymour arrived at a little cottage. Belle could see a village in the distance, but her focus remained on the house. "Gorgeous," she whispered. She rubbed the temples of her forehead, trying to remember her home. But recalling nothing, Belle gave up, telling herself that she hit her head too hard to remember anything.

Seymour cleared his throat as he helped Belle down from the saddle. "Belle, dear, would you mind putting Philippe away in the barn? He has missed you, so I think the two of you should spend some time together." The man quickly pulled out two lumps of sugar. "If you give him these, I think he will forgive your absence."

The girl took the sweets and ran off, laughing as Philippe trotted behind her.

Seymour sighed as he turned to enter the cottage. Even after five years, the place still felt cold and barren. Since his wife had died, the house had seemed to recess into a dormant atmosphere. Seymour sighed again. Looking out one of the many dusty windows, he smiled as he saw Belle frolicking in the field, giggling as the sugar-craving horse chased her around. *"Maybe this little girl will bring some light into our lives."*

Seymour slowly walked to a tiny room in the back of the house. The door was slightly opened, but the man did not walk in right away; he knocked and waited for a reply.

"Come in, Papa." A tiny voice rang out from behind the door.

Seymour opened the door and cautiously entered the room. There, by the only clean window in the house, stood a girl. She was small and frail for a girl of twelve-years-old, but she had the most caring heart of anyone Seymour had ever known. But even when Seymour had been standing in the room for a few moments, his daughter still gazed out the window.

"Lilly, I –"

"Who is she, Papa?"

"At least she is still talking to me." Seymour sat down on the edge of Lily's bed, positioning himself in a what-I-have-to-say-is-difficult position. Bending forward, Seymour clasped his hands together and continued. "She's a girl that I found in the woods. She was alone and does not have many memories of who she is and where she belongs. She . . . she thinks she is part of our family."

Lilly's shoulders slumped, but she made no other move of acknowledgement.

"Dear, I know this will be hard on us both, but I think we need to take her in as though she always belonged here –"

Lilly quickly turned and threw herself at her father. Tightly wrapping her skinny arms around his neck, the girl whispered, "Thank you," over and over again. Seymour's face was instantly showered with kisses and joyful tears as Lilly cried, "I have always wanted a sister!" Even though Seymour was taken aback, he soon reciprocated and wrapped one arm around his daughter and stroked her flaxen hair with his hand. In a moment of silence, Seymour and Lilly did nothing but hold each other's steady gaze. That instant, they both knew that they were ready for their lives to change. Lilly smiled and rushed to the door to greet her lost sister.

Chapter Five
Birth of the Beast

The castle was now colder than ever. The only life that occupied the stony halls was a brute and a monster. The structure and design of the castle had changed. The once tall, light-inviting windows had been boarded up with wood and glazed over with spider webs. Angels and statues of saints had turned into hideous gargoyles and demon-like figures. The fires gave no more comforting warmth; instead, they played with one's mind as they cast eerie shadows upon the walls. The only breath that could be heard was the ragged, vehement grunts of the monster.

Standing in his relic's room, Adam surveyed his spoils of war. The warriors who had not been killed in battle were able to deliver the plunder of the conquest to the castle before being sent to their homes. As a remembrance, the prince had hung up the wings and bloody armor of all the fairies that he and his warriors had killed.

The prince had hung the queen's wings in the center of the room, the pinnacle of his victory. He had seen to her death personally. Leaning against the locked door, Adam sighed and closed his eyes; a wicked smile spread across his weary face as he recalled the last events of the gory night.

Six Months Prior

Three swords, one woman. Adam knew that there was no conceivable way for his last victim to escape. With Vicenti and another soldier behind the fairy, Adam knelt in front of the queen. Nodding, the men pushed the fairy down to their prince's level. Holding his sword in front of her chest, Adam whispered, "You have a minute to live, your *highness*. Repent, and I shall assure you a painless death."

"Why should I repent?"

"You . . . you, Queen Jezé, had my parents murdered. I have been waiting for two years, waiting for the day when I could drain your blood and the blood of your people as recompense. Now," Adam grabbed the fairy's shoulder, pulling her closer to the tip of his blade, "Any last requests?"

The queen scoffed, a cold fire burning in her eyes. "Do you think I am afraid of your threats? I am a conquering queen, one whose army has taken over many villages. I am a queen who does not tolerate weakness. When my husband had become weak in his misery and grief, claiming a peaceful life was the only life to live, I had him killed. I am a queen who has seen more death, more battles, and more bloodshed than you could ever imagine. Now tell me, why should I be afraid of you? You are just a frightened *boy*, trying to kill like a man."

Adam slowly broke off his eye contact with Jezé and nodded at the soldier behind her. With a calculated downward stroke, the sword severed through the fairy's wings. Adam looked back at the queen, who was silently screaming in pain. Her onyx eyes were overwhelmed with tears. Burying her shoulder into Adam's palm, the queen kept herself from crumpling to the floor. As her dress was slicked with blood, she choked out, "Who are you, boy? I have orphaned many children in my crusades; why are you the only one that has come for revenge?" Her words were labored, and after she forced out what she had to say, Jezé filled the cavernous hall with her pain-filled scream. One hundred tortured souls could have screamed, but they would not have been able to drown out the anguished and echoing cry of the queen.

Adam grinned, taking great satisfaction in the fairy's pain. After waiting until Jezé had drained her energy, he lifted her head with the tip of his sword. "Because you did not only murder my parents, but also the monarchs of France. And as the heir of King Avery, I have a sworn duty to revenge my father's life."

At this, the fairy began to convulse, screaming more wildly than before. "No! No, he . . . they told me everyone was killed! No one survived! How could you have escaped the wolves?"

Adam twirled the hilt of his sword around in his hand, gently scraping the queen's ivory chin. "One silent death of a wolf allowed me the opportunity to leave." Squaring his shoulders and tilting his head back in an air of command, the prince spoke, "Queen Jezé, I hereby charge you with the conspiracy to commit murder and being the leader in an act of treason. I sentence you to death!"

The queen's screams of protest were grotesquely cut short as Adam pulled his sword away from her throat and rammed the blade through Jezé's chest. Jezé gasped once for breath and then crumpled on the floor. Her face contorted; her ivory skin began to turn the shade of icy death. Adam stared at the body, watching as her life and blood spilled in a similar way as that of his parents. He began to feel that his revenge was complete.

"What should we do with the body, sir?" Vicenti interrupted. Even though he was a long-time general, he had never seen a battle end in the cruel murder of a woman. His stomach soured as he watched the cold, heartless prince roughly nudge the body with the tip of his boot. "Sir?"

"Leave her here. Grab the wings. Oh, and burn the building."

Adam had hoped that the victory would settle his soul and maybe fill the hole in his heart, but nothing helped. Adam gripped a table's ledge to steady himself. His head pounded with pain. His heart pumped anger, a lethal poison, into his veins. The prince bit his lip so hard that blood started to seep out of the broken skin. He brushed his shaking hand against his lip and stared at the glossy, red liquid that painted his fingertips. He had spilled so much fairy blood that night in hopes of requiting the blood of his parents. Apparently, Adam's victory in battle had not been enough; the emotional pain still throbbed.

Adam's arm twitched and his head rolled back. *"Insolent fairy. I can feel her curse beginning to take control."* Thankfully, she no longer posed as a threat. She was dead. Then Adam began to think back, back to the time when he began to pursue Enchantress. Had he not seen two fairies run for the forest's cover? He had only killed one. What of the other?

As he paced the room, Adam casually reached his hand into one of his jacket's pockets. He was shocked to feel a little package. Remembering that Enchantress had placed something in the same pocket before she died, Adam pulled out the parcel. In his hand laid an irregularly shaped glass; the glass glowed with a dim light and was of the purest substance Adam had ever seen. Looking through the shard, Adam saw so clearly that he believed he could see the world. He sat the piece on a table and turned his attention to the paper that had been wrapped around the glass fragment. Adam was shocked to find that there was writing on the parchment, and after lighting a candle, he began to read in a frenzied state.

As Prophetess of this sect of Fairae Land, I often receive strange visions and revelations. Just a fortnight ago, I saw, in my dreams, a young boy. This boy was in pain, and he released his pain through acts of hatred. His name was, in the human tongue, Adam. I am writing this letter in his language, because I know he will read this, and he will need to understand my letter's meaning.

In this dream, I also saw my own death. I died by the hand of this boy. As recompense for his deeds, Adam will be turned into a Beast, so as to help him realize what his heart appears to be. Do not dishearten, for there is hope, young Adam! There will come a time, when you are older, a young princess, Sabella Rose, will hold the key to your transformation. Show the girl that your heart can change, and you will turn back to your human self.

I also give you my prized possession: my mirror. To you, my treasure may look simple and unworthy to be in a prince's proprietorship. I have, however, spoken over this mirror such a blessing, that the shard is no longer a mere piece of glass; perhaps you have already noticed how clear it is, clearer than any man-made mirror of which you have knowledge. Speak to my mirror whenever you wish. Learn to speak politely, and my little piece of glass will show you whatever you long to see, except anything concerning Sabella Rose; I desire you to be surprised when she arrives. I do not want you to know what she looks like, who she is in this life, or when she will arrive at your castle. I only ask you to trust my words. She will come.

Be warned. The girl will not last forever; like a wilting flower, she will surely fade. If you do not perform the tasks you need to complete before she wilts away at the blossoming age of nineteen, she will die. You will be left to forever be a monster.

This was my dream.

Enchantress

Prophetess and Queen of the Green Fairae Isles

Adam crumpled up the paper and threw his written doom to the floor. Why was he to be forced to lower himself to a fairy's demands? Why should have to ask forgiveness? The fairies killed his parents, and they turned him into . . . what exactly was he turning into?

The prince ran to his bedroom. Along the way, he found himself thrashing at the walls, yelling inhumanly, and stumbling. In a fit of rage, Adam lunged at one of the statues hanging from the wall, aiming for the gargoyle's head. As he ran on, Adam glanced over his shoulder to see that the miniature beast had been decapitated. *"Did I do that?"*

Once reaching his room, the prince slammed the doors shut and locked himself away. *"Must find a mirror."* Adam turned to find his full-length mirror to the right of him.

Before him, in his own reflection, stood a horrendous beast of terrifying proportions. He could almost recognize his human figure, but he noticed he was taller and broader about the shoulders. His spine had risen, and his back hunched slightly. The monster's arms had gained muscles, and his hands had grown larger as well; sharp, claw-like nails began curving off each finger. His hair, with a mess of tangles and knots, now flowed raggedly about his shoulders. But his new mass of hair could not hide his face.

The monster's eyes were almost black, and they showed no mercy or warmth. Scars plagued his cheeks and forehead, and his nose had become reflective of an animal. His skin was abnormally pale and was now thinly stretched over his pronounced bones. And the fangs! White ivory fangs forced their way out of the monster's mouth, and they glistened like scythes waiting to be used in gory battle. Stepping back, Adam saw that he was no longer a man, but a monster.

"*What would Chip think if he saw me now?*" The thought overwhelmed Adam, causing him to crumple to the ground and moan. Even his cries and sobs were not the sounds of a boy, but of an injured animal. His tears, though, were the same. "*How could I have been so cold? Why did I think that I could ever live without love?*" Adam knew that he was ready to change his heart, but his body would have to wait. Adam paced around his room, wondering when this Sabella Rose would decide to show herself.

Chapter Six

A Strange Feeling

    The years passed on. The sisterly bond between Lilly and Belle grew stronger every day, as if their relationship had always been. Lilly taught Belle how to read (Seymour explained that Belle's fall had reverted her back to a preschool level of understanding). Belle easily adapted to her "new" home, fitting in as though she never left. The girl did not seem to mind that she had no memories, for she was resolved to make her own.

    But Seymour was the one who had the most difficult challenge. He had to figure how to explain to an entire village that he suddenly had two daughters! He started with Monsieur Cartier Chantelle, the village doctor. Seymour knew that if he could convince the doctor and his wife (who was the biggest gossip around) that Belle really was his daughter, everything would fall into place. Therefore, Seymour took Belle to meet the good doctor.

    "And who might this be?" Cartier chimed as he opened the door of his house. Seymour Dubois he knew, but the girl was unrecognizable.

"Monsieur Cartier, this is Belle, my eldest daughter." Seymour mouthed the words, "Humor her," as he caught the doctor's curious eyes.

"Oh, Papa, you can be such a teaser. Monsieur Cartier knows me!" After two years, Belle had fitted herself into her new life unknowingly. She had Lilly help her to remember all the people's names in the village. Belle never once considered herself a stranger. Even though Belle never met the doctor, the young woman walked into the house as though she had been there a hundred times.

"Uh, Belle, of course I know you! You have matured into such a beautiful young woman, I hardly recognized you! Why don't you take a quick visit to our powder room before I start the examination?" Cartier watched as Belle sweetly nodded and turned to walk down the single hall. After waiting to hear the door shut, Cartier turned on Seymour. "Seymour, how —"

"I know this is a confusing situation," the man interrupted. Peering over the doctor's shoulder to make sure that his daughter was still occupied, Seymour continued, "I found this girl in the woods a few years ago. Her head was injured and she had no memories. She was alone, but she seemed to believe that I was her father. I treat her as my eldest, and I ask that you and everyone else do the same."

"And you have kept her hidden this entire time?"

Seymour shook his head. "Not exactly. I did for the majority of the first year, telling her that she needed to rest her head and not over exert herself. In all honesty, I was waiting to see if anyone came to claim her. But no one came, so I let her have free roam; she has even visited the village a couple of times."

Cartier laughed and then hushed his voice. "My wife has talked about a strange girl who wanders the village like a ghost and who addresses everyone with ease. She described this girl as, 'a gangly little thing that has no emotion,' but I now see she has exaggerated. So why have you come to me?"

"I need your help to," Seymour scratched his unshaven chin, trying to find words. "I need your help to spread the word. Everyone in this place trusts the words of the Cartier house. Maybe, if you are the one convincing them, the people will really believe she is my daughter. Perhaps a daughter that has been missing for quite some time. Kidnapped, maybe? I don't want Belle to grow up feeling out of place."

As the two men waited, Seymour noticed a small painting of the monarchs hanging on the doctor's wall. He smiled sadly as he surveyed the lovely faces of the king and queen, the dear departed. Their remains had been found in the woods, tragically mauled by wolves. No one really knew what had become of the prince; the village had witnessed his coronation. The boy king ruled for all of two years before disappearing. He had rallied a small army, conducted a battle, but had not been heard of since. Some assumed him dead, others believed he still lived alone in his castle. Seymour began to wonder how much longer their country could go without a monarchy guiding them through the ages; quite a few people were very pleased there were no more rulers and threatened to revolt if the monarchy revived.

  At that moment, Belle skipped back towards her father and the doctor. "I'm ready, Doctor Cartier."

  Cartier led Belle into a room that was directly off the foyer. Belle was taken aback by how clean the room was! She had seen sketches of doctors' offices in books; they were all cluttered and cramped, but Monsieur Cartier's office was near perfection. There were no pill bottles lying haphazardly on desks with their bead-like contents spilling out. Not a single tool was misplaced or dirty. Cartier had everything organized! The room was not dark as Belle had expected. No, the room was brightly lit, lightly painted, and felt very welcoming.

  In the center of the room was a tall, thin table. Belle assumed this is where she was supposed to go. She hoisted herself up onto the table and Monsieur Cartier began the examination. He was delighted and astounded by the fact that Belle never ran out of things to say. First, she would ask questions, then she would explain her questions in stories, and then she would ask different questions related to the stories she told. Finally, when Belle was in a rare few moments of silence, the doctor asked her some questions of his own.

"Belle, forgive me if I have asked you this before, but do you like to read?"

"Oh yes, sir! Papa says my reading time is the only time when I am completely silent. But I love books; they expound my knowledge and spark my curiosity." Belle's smile faded into a disappointed sigh, "But I've read all our books at home, and Papa says we must spend what little money we have on better things."

"Do you remember my little bookshop in the village?"

"Of course!" Belle really did not remember, though. There had been many incidents since her return where she was asked, "Do you remember this," and she usually agreed, letting others fix her memories one piece at a time.

"Now that you are back, why don't you come by sometime? I just got quite a few more books, all new and ready to be read."

Belle eagerly agreed.

"You know, my nephew is coming to town in a few days. I would like you to meet him. He's never had a love for books, but perhaps your appreciation for literature will inspire him."

"I'd be honored to be an ambassador for literature, Doctor." With that, and a parting handshake, Belle walked out to meet with her father.

"She's perfectly healthy, Seymour. There is not a single after shock or side effect from concussion. I would like to see every four months, just so I can monitor her pretty head."

Seymour acknowledged the doctor, but his eyes remained on Belle. She smiled and stood gracefully by his side, but there seemed to be a sorrowful burden, a sort of weariness, lurking in her eyes. Her countenance appeared to be a façade; a curtain trying to cover a secret thought perhaps? Seymour put a hold on his suspicions as he escorted Belle out the door.

"Belle, I have some errands I need to run. Would you like to come with me or go home?"

"I think I'd like to go home, Papa. I will see you later." Belle stood on her tiptoes and gently kissed her father's cheek. Once home, Belle felt herself being pulled to her bed. Not bothering to even remove her shoes, Belle collapsed on the bed and let out a tired sigh. She had almost felt this way before, but the pain had never been as intense. What was happening to her?

"Belle! You are home early. I thought you would still be out with Papa. Is anything wrong?"

Too weary to cry, Belle just moaned. "Everything is wrong, Lilly."

Lilly moved closer and gently sat herself on the bed beside her sister. Lovingly stroking Belle's hair, she took a few strands and began to braid. "Really, Belle. *Everything?* What specifically is wrong?"

"I'm wrong! At least, my body is. I feel like I am wilting from the inside out. Chains of loathsome dreariness weigh upon my shoulders. I feel cold. And tired."

"Did you talk to Doctor Cartier about this?"

"No. I did not feel like bringing up the subject. I was prepared, if anything was found, to talk freely about the irregularities that I have felt. But he found nothing wrong!"

"Might your pain might be . . . imaginary?"

Belle shrugged, which even took some effort. "If so, I have a splendid, yet overworking, mind. Lilly," Belle turned her head towards her sister, tears still refusing to come, "I feel like I am dying."

"Maybe we should talk to Papa about this."

"I couldn't, Lilly. I do not want him worrying about possibly losing me." Belle weakly smiled and pulled herself up into a sitting position, letting out a sigh of relief; she was beginning to feel better. Perhaps she had just experienced a moment of strong fatigue. She prayed that she would never have to feel the pain she had just endured, the hopelessness of an impending death, but something inside told Belle that the discomfort she suffered would indeed return and would play a bigger role in her life. Consenting to only focus on how she felt at the moment, well and rested, Belle invited Lilly into the kitchen as the two sisters prepared the night's meal.

Chapter Seven
Cartier's Nephew

Over the next couple of days, Lilly and Belle worked at putting Belle's mysterious pain in the past. In fact, they never brought up the day of the doctor visit. One night, while her sister was braiding her hair, Belle remembered that she wanted to discuss a certain young man with Lilly.

"Back in the doctor's room, Cartier said he has a nephew who will be visiting soon."

Lilly's eyes brightened slightly and emotion gleefully tugged at the corners of her smile. "I have met him before, but only briefly. His name is Caspar Liárd and he is about your age. He lives in the Province of Guyenne and Gascony with his parents, but he comes to visit his relatives here every few months or so." Lilly's voice seemed to trail off, and a slight smile played about her lips.

"But you've only met him once?" Belle asked, a hint of mischievousness in her voice.

"Well, met him once," continued Lilly, completely ignoring her sister's playful tone. "I have seen him a few times. In the distance, that is."

Belle jumped off her bed and swung around to face her sister, whose hands hung in the air as though she was still braiding. Belle put her hands on her hips. "Lilly Charlotte Dubois, I do believe you are in love!"

"That's complete nonsense! Now sit back down and let me finish your braid."

"I won't move until you give me an answer. Are you, or are you not, in love with Caspar Liárd? I have never heard you speak of any boy so affectionately."

Lilly pursed her lips. "I refuse to answer that question, Belle, simply because no matter what I answer, it will be twisted!"

"How so?"

"If I answer no, you will call me a liar. If I answer yes, then I *know* I will be lying."

"I understand, Lilly. So, you are not attracted to him; who cares one way or another? He's probably a pig-faced monster anyhow." Belle pushed up her nose, crossed her eyes, and started to snort. This made Lilly fall on the bed in a fit of giggles and roll around.

"Oh no," Lilly cried, "It's the Fairy Gobbler!"

Now Belle was the one to laugh. The Fairy Gobbler was a creature she had invented as her way of accounting for the loss of the fairy population. She and Lilly would always laugh and make jokes about the monster, going on pretend adventures to seek out and destroy the creature. But something inside Belle knew this was not something to laugh at or make light. She felt there had been a monster that ravaged the countryside, destroying all fairies. *"Perhaps he still lives."*

As promised, Belle stopped by Monsieur Cartier's bookshop every day. Cartier understood that Belle did not have the funds to buy enough books to satisfy her ever-expanding knowledge, so he made her a deal: for every book she borrowed, Belle would have to learn something applicable to life. She would then report to Cartier and, in detail, explain what she had learned.

Belle loved the bookshop. To her, the little two-room store was a sparkling diamond amidst lumps of coal. In the entire village, she needed no other shop's wares like she needed the books. Belle did not need the bakery; Lilly was a supreme cook and baker. She did not need the dress shop or tailor's store, for the Dubois' wardrobe was never extravagant. But as she grew older and wiser, Belle knew she needed the bookshop.

Every day, as Belle approached the shop, she would first study the door. She had completely memorized the surface of the door; she knew every chip of paint, every crack, and every splinter on the cherry red door, but still she studied it. She enjoyed making sure nothing had changed. Then Belle would enter the shop, feeling peace as if it was her second home. She would then sit in a chair by the window and read. Sometimes she would hear the village women passing by, clicking their tongues, and gossiping about how Belle should take her head out of those books, but the girl never minded. She took comfort in what she read, especially the older books.

"Belle! I just received a new shipment of books. Feel free to look them over. They are in a box," Cartier announced as Belle walked into the shop.

"*Merci*. I will." Belle easily found the box and immediately began to look through the contents. Twenty-one books in all, but the first twenty did not captivate Belle. The last book, however, was special. The cover was a dark, mahogany red, which was a stunning contrast to the book's ivory pages. The spine was bound well and the pages turned with ease. The lettering on the front was what intrigued Belle the most.

In a tint of gold, the words "Fairy Tales" flowed across the book's cover, but there was nothing else! There was no more fancy script anywhere on the outside of the book, nor was there any explanation as to what a fairy tale was.

"*Perhaps*," Belle thought to herself, "*Perhaps this book is an account of the fairies' history.*"

Belle quickly put all the other books in the box. Lifting her skirts and rising to leave, Belle called out, "I found my book! I'll bring it next week as promised." As Belle turned to rush for the door, she realized she was moving too fast to prevent a head-on collision with a boy coming through the door.

Once she had broken out of her daze, Belle looked up to see the boy's worried face staring at her. "Dear me! Are you alright?"

"Dear *you*? I was the one that fell," Belle quipped.

"Ah, but I was the one you ran into," the boy laughed as he extended his hand down towards Belle. "I must say I would have felt better if I had the door fall down on me!"

Belle's laugh chimed out as she took his hand, finding herself effortlessly lifted off the floor. She then also took notice of the boy, who was nearly a man; he had firm hands, piercing eyes, and proud stature. "*No wonder you spoke about him so caringly, Lilly,*" Belle thought to herself. She brushed off her dress and cleared her throat. "You must be Caspar." Belle extended her hand in greeting.

"Beautiful *and* wise. You must be Belle." Caspar grasped Belle's hand and pressed his lips gently upon her knuckles. The maiden quickly raised her other hand to her cheeks, which were most likely the same color as her fairy book. Caspar looked into her eyes, and for the shortest moments, Belle was positively sure that every living creature had vanished; only Caspar and she remained in a world of their own.

She was, for a moment, overwhelmed with fear, and another unexplainable feeling; she was afraid at the thought that her heart could be won over by love so easily. But should she really constitute this feeling as love? She knew what father-daughter love felt like, as well as sisterly love, but she didn't know how to describe the feeling a girl gets when she loves her prince, her future husband.

But something deep inside told her that this was not love. She had heard of her father speak of infatuation; was this feeling, this light-headed, heart-pounding, mind-numbing sensation only infatuation? Belle wasn't sure one way or the other, but she knew that if Caspar was trying to win her heart, he'd have to do more than simply kiss her hand.

The boy was the first to break the silence. "So, you take a liking in fairy tale books."

"Books?" Belle spoke in the present, but absently, because her mind was in the other moment. "Oh! Books, yes, I take a great liking in them. Do you?"

Caspar shook his head, and his dark curls bounced as he did. "Not particularly. If I may be so bold, I do not really care for fables and fantasies. A bit childish for people our age, don't you think?"

"Oh no," Belle quickly replied, trying to hide her disappointment. "In fact, I don't even believe these are fables. Now they are not as soundproof as the Holy Bible, but I do believe they are a part of history."

"I see. Perhaps you are right, Belle. You have a most intellectually stimulating theory; you could have a brilliant idea in that beautiful head of yours."

"You truly believe so?" Belle felt herself swell with pride at the thought of her theory being accepted; everyone else, except Lilly, mocked her beliefs.

"Indeed I do. Now, I think my uncle wants me in the back with him. Might we see one another again?"

"I think that would be fine. I shall discuss this with my family, but would your family and you like to come to dinner tomorrow night?"

As Caspar walked Belle out the door, he asked, "Must I wait so long? But yes, I would be delighted."

After watching Belle disappear far down the road, Caspar walked into the back room to meet with his uncle. After hashing over details of his trip, Caspar talked with his uncle about Belle. "Don't you think her fairy theory is a little ridiculous? Preposterous, even?"

Cartier shrugged. "Caspar, Belle has had a nearly traumatic childhood. She will most likely grow out of these beliefs. I would be careful about criticizing how she thinks; Belle is a very sensitive girl, but she backs up her beliefs with a passion. If you wish to win her heart, you must accept her as she is, and not how you want her to be."

Chapter Eight
Visions and Monsters

"This is a fabulous dinner," Mademoiselle Louise Chantelle cooed as she, her husband, and Caspar sat with the Dubois family at an old oak table. Caspar had informed her of Belle's invite, but Louise had been skeptical of the quality of the dinner's outcome. Louise did not consider herself to assume the worst of others, but seeing the poverty that Seymour and his girls lived in, she assumed that they would not receive a decent meal. Louise knew that she had to be polite, so she tried the food, and became pleasantly surprised.

"Thank you, Louise," Seymour replied. "But don't praise me. The girls wouldn't even let me in the kitchen."

"And don't consider me the chef of the family," Belle interjected. "I was Lilly's helper and that is all. She concocted these recipes, arranged the menu, and cooked the dishes herself!"

Lilly smiled, but did not reply to Mademoiselle Chantelle's accolades; she kept her head down. She had been quiet throughout the dinner, because she could not stop thinking about Belle and Caspar. Belle had come the other day and explained their chance meeting, but she mentioned nothing of love or the desire to marry. But now Lilly saw everything plainly; Caspar had a look on his face of a young man in love, but Belle was coy, probably not wanting to hand over her heart so easily. If Lilly was the one in Belle's place, she would willingly return Caspar's affections. But seeing the dreaming, far-away look in the boy's eyes, Lilly knew that she never had a chance of being Madam Liárd.

She was almost okay with that fact. Lilly knew that she was not a ravishing beauty like Belle; she had soft, white skin and sparkling eyes, but that was all that she considered beautiful about herself. Lilly knew that she was not as bright of a conversationalist as Belle was, but even though her words were few, Lilly believed them to be meaningful and wise. Belle did constantly rave over Lilly's writings. Lilly also thought she was an excellent cook (tonight's dinner was an example). However, she did not believe a single one of her skills was valuable to her at the moment; there was nothing she could do or say that would draw Caspar's attention to her. Maybe her destiny was to stay overshadowed by Belle.

"I'm going to the kitchen," Belle explained as she rose from her chair. "Is there anything that I may get for anyone?"

"I would like some more water," Cartier kindly asked.

Belle agreed and after giving a final call for requests, she headed to the kitchen. Lilly knew she should offer to help, but she wanted to talk to Caspar. "If *I can calm my nerves,*" she thought. Taking a deep breath, telling herself there was nothing to be nervous about, Lilly opened her mouth to speak, but was interrupted by the sound of a pitcher breaking. After no reassurance from Belle, everyone got up from the table to see what had happened. Lilly began to cry as they all entered the kitchen.

Belle lay on the floor, crumpled and shaking. The broken remains of the pitcher surrounded one of her hands, the spilled water soaking into her sleeve. A small trickle of blood pooled around her head, mixing eerily with the puddle of water. The men gathered beside unconscious Belle, while Louise held Lilly close. Tears were hiding in everyone's eyes, but Lilly knew she felt the worst. Just moments ago, she had been near to resenting her sister for stealing Caspar's heart; now she was hit with the realization that life was too short for her to form any grudges.

Cartier left quickly to fetch his tools and medicines while Seymour and Caspar carried Belle to the bedroom. After Belle had been gently arranged on her bed, Lilly asked if they could be alone until Doctor Cartier arrived. Lilly waited until the door was closed before approaching the bed. Tears flowing freely, Lilly chocked out her apology.

"Belle, I don't know if you can hear me, but I am truly sorry for even entertaining the thought of jealousy in my mind. I wanted Caspar, but if he is the man you are to marry . . . I will be very happy for you both." The girl then bent down and lightly kissed Belle's forehead.

"Lilly?" Belle asked softly a few minutes later. She tried to sit up, but her pounding headache convinced her that she should just stay down. "How long have I been this way?"

Lilly grasped Belle's hands, which were strangely cold. As thankful tears streamed down her cheeks, she replied, "Only for fifteen minutes or so. Monsieur Cartier went to his office to bring the things he needs. Papa insists that you receive a thorough examination." The girl stayed silent for a moment, and then decided that she could not hold back her curiosity. "Belle, what caused this?"

Belle heaved a sigh of confusion. "I don't know. I remember getting up from the table and then going to the kitchen. I went outside to fill the pitcher, and then came immediately back inside." Belle paused as her body began to shiver. "I remember becoming strangely fixated on the kitchen window. I . . . I saw something."

Lilly leaned in closely. "What did you see, Belle?"

"Well, I saw many things. First, I saw my own reflection; I was slightly older and . . . and surrounded by wolves. I knew they were going to attack, but something stopped them, something protected me. Next, I saw a castle, one that was abandoned and death-like. Lastly, I saw a woman; she wore a beautiful dress, but the midsection had been badly torn. I believe I saw dried blood." Belle's breath became labored as she realized how real everything had felt. "She held a rose in her right hand, one like I have never seen before. The rose glowed with beauty, but it was quickly dying. The woman stretched out her hands and said, 'Your time is coming; prepare yourself.' I believe that's when I fainted."

Lilly shuddered as she rubbed her chilled arms. "That would make anyone faint. Do you think you saw a ghost?"

"Nonsense. Ghosts do not exist. I do think I could have seen a vision; maybe pieces of the future, some of the past, maybe even the present."

A tender knock on the door interrupted the girls' conversation. Monsieur Cartier was back and ready to start his examination. Lilly kindly bowed out of the room, all the while pondering Belle's vision. She did not believe in ghosts either, but to think that Belle saw that complex of a vision also stretched her mind and perturbed her soul. Moreover, why that vision? None of those pictures pertained to her life as of now.

"*But what about her life before now?*" Belle and she had grown so close that Lilly would sometimes forget that Belle had another life before she became a part of the Dubois family. Who had she been, and did her vision pertain to who she once was? Lilly kept all her thoughts to herself. She did not know if she was overthinking things, but Belle's vision kept her pondering throughout the night.

Adam sat alone in his garden, the only place where he felt peace. Not that he could call the place a garden anymore; the bushes, which had grown as high as walls, were now overgrown and covered in choking ivy. Thorns were abundant and the grass had all died. The monster did not mind the dreariness; actually, the garden's ugliness rather pleased him. He would prowl the labyrinth of hedges, playing a tasty game of hide-and-seek with unsuspecting birds. The thorns were tolerable because the soles of his feet had become so tough and leathery that he barely noticed the miniature spikes. Yes, the Beast was pleased with his garden.

Contrarily, Adam was not. As he sat on one of the stone benches, he recalled all the times that his family would spend here. His mother, dressed in her silken, peach-colored gowns, would stroll around and whisper to the flowers as though they were bosom friends. When Adam was very young, he would imagine that the flowers would talk back, each according to its own personality. The prince also recalled the times he had spent with his father in the garden. They would always play and chase each other around the bushes, much to the amusement of the queen. Sometimes they would even act unnecessarily silly, making noises at the birds and rolling around on the grass.

That was a long while ago. Adam had just recently turned seventeen, and the monster inside of him told Adam to forget all memories of past childhood joy. "They keep me alive." Adam whispered to the Beast. He understood that he was talking to himself, but he was not ready to admit that monster and man were one.

"*They hold you back.*" The monster would growl.

"My parents loved me."

"*How many times did they abandon you at the castle?*"

"I must remember my parents. The fairy said that I must change my heart if I am to change back to who I was. Surely focusing on love will help me."

"*Change back if you want, but there really wasn't, and isn't, a difference. Think about this. Think of the hurt in Timothy's eyes when we yelled at him for the fifth time in the same day. Think about how shocked Estelle was when we called her a hideous whore. Think of how even Mrs. Agatha*

Kettlery would not even come near us. We were a monster then, we are a monster now."

"Then maybe I am not supposed to change back. Maybe I am supposed to change for the better; change into a different man completely."

"NO! I will not let you change. We are one; I cannot survive without you. You cannot survive without me. I am your rage. I am your inner monster. If you change, if you get rid of me, you will not be yourself anymore. You will not be whole. You will die! No, I won't let you change."

Adam's shoulders began to shake uncontrollably. His hands clenched, his overgrown claws digging into the stone bench. Every day the monster's rage grew stronger, poisoning the prince's heart and mind more and more. Adam ran back inside the castle, back to his bedroom, and back to his mirror. He, once a day, would stare at the reflecting glass and watch himself transform.

Today, he noticed that his muscles started to unnaturally bulge, causing the flesh to rip in some places. The fine hair on his arms had grown to be as long and as matted as the hair on his head; he looked like a savage hunter who hid under the fur hides of his prey. *"We might be separate now,"* Adam thought to himself, *"But soon there will not be enough man to resist the monster; only a Beast there will forever be."*

Now, I know you might think that this is a strange situation. How can Adam be in one form, yet have two separate identities raging on at the same time? So understand this: Adam, at this time, is still Adam, only he is hideously disfigured. But his hate, which has been growing inside of him since the night of his parents' death, is turning him into a real monster. You see, Enchantress did not give Adam the power to the hate; she just made Adam's outward appearance reflect his heart. Sometimes we cannot visualize how horrific our inward thoughts are unless we have the opportunity to see what others are seeing. Adam, who now really looks like the monster his hate wishes him to be, can finally understand how Chip and the others felt when the prince would rant or rage. This is the key to Adam's transformation. I shall not give anymore away; you will have to read for yourself. We shall now move on another two years.

Chapter Nine
The Inventor

"What do you mean, Papa? You've what?" Belle stood in the tiny kitchen with a chipped dish in one hand and a holey dishtowel in the other. Her father had just come home, his face flushed with excitement and his eyes sparkling with childish glee.

"Belle, I've quit my job!"

The dish promptly slipped from Belle's hand and, quite loudly, shattered on the floor. Belle used her freed hand to steady herself on a nearby counter. Now seventeen, Belle had taken on the responsibility of taking care of the Dubois' house. Even though Belle would never admit this to her father, she found the challenge to be difficult enough with only Seymour's small income and her less than noteworthy salary; now that she had even less to work with, Belle knew she would have to find another job.

Belle felt herself slowly sink down to the floor, falling into numb state of mind as well. She started to pick up the pieces of the plate, but her tears began to blur her vision. Exasperated and ashamed, Belle buried her head in the towel.

"Oh, Papa! Why? Delivering packages was not that horrible. The job paid decently –"

"This had nothing to do with how the job was or the pay. Belle, I had no more passion for riding across the land, just to give a few people their letters and packages. And when you don't have any more passion, you appear to be a bad employee." Seymour bent down and pulled Belle close, cradling her head. "I knew I would have been fired soon. Besides, Philippe is getting old; he can't travel like he used to when he was young."

"So what are we going to do now?" Belle pushed herself off her father's chest so that she could look into his eyes. "Papa, if need be, I can get another job. I am sure there is something else I could do for Doctor Cartier."

At that, Seymour smiled the happiest grin that Belle had ever seen. Slowly beginning to stand, Seymour said, "Belle, you don't have to get another job. I've already received an offer."

"You have?" Belle rose to her feet as well. *"There was never anything to worry about."*

Grabbing his daughter's hand, Seymour led Belle out of the house and to the side of the cottage. Stopping at the entrance to the old cellar, Seymour instructed Belle to close her eyes; laughing incredulously, Belle finally did as she was told. Belle shook her head when her father asked if she could see anything. "Just to be sure," mumbled Seymour. Belle began to protest as she felt her father tying a piece of fabric around her eyes.

"Papa!"

"I just want the surprise to be real."

So Belle relaxed and listened. The cellar door groaned like a man who had not risen from his bed in decades. Seymour took Belle's hand once again and guided her down the stairs, which creaked in response to the newly applied weight. As Belle descended, she tried not to think of the many creatures that were now scurrying away, or of the cobwebs that were clinging to her hair. Carefully inhaling, Belle was greeted by a freshly cleaned scent, not the old and musty stench that she thought would be in the room. After hearing the scratch of matches, Belle begged that the blindfold be removed.

"Alright. You can open your eyes."

As the cloth slipped down off her face, the young woman gasped in shock. The room was not playing the part of a rusty cellar anymore, but Belle could not decide what the room was supposed to be. There was hay everywhere; some straws were loosely covering the floor, and others were tied into bales and were being used to pad three walls. On the fourth wall was a large fireplace, containing an already lit fire. Tools were lying on benches and gears were thrown into barrels. There was a large pile of wood in the corner and a mound of rocks and stones in the other.

After taking two or three good looks around the room, Belle shrugged and turned back to her father. "Okay, Papa, I give up. What have you done to the cellar and what does your knew job have to do with this?"

"Belle, I have become an inventor!"

Belle was sure that if there had been another dish in her hand, that dish too would have been broken. "That's . . . wonderful, Papa. If that has become your passion, I am sure Lilly and I will support you fully. But, how well does that pay?"

"The job of an inventor will pay marvelously, as soon as one comes up with a worthy invention. Take that gentleman in Italy, for instance. He invented the piano a few decades ago, and I bet he received quite a bit of money. Or what about the person who invented the steam engine, or the thermometer, or –"

Belle smiled as she listened to her father rave on about the famous inventors of their time. She was proud to see her father so joyful over his new "job." However, she also realized that the pay would not be as lucrative as he imagined.

"*I will need to get another job,*" Belle decided, but she would not tell her father. Belle understood the pride that he took in his work, and how crushed that pride would be if he found out that his daughter was the main provider for the family. Belle just kept on smiling, believing that everything was going to be fine.

"And the best part, Belle, is that I will have a yearly opportunity to sell my inventions. I met a man today that informed me of a village not too far from here that has a fair every fall; they ask new inventors to come and display their works. I thought that the fair would be a perfect start to my new career. So, I gave the man the entrance fee and I will now be expected to appear at the fair."

Belle found herself overwhelmed by the words, "entrance fee." Proceeding tentatively, Belle asked, "How much of an entrance fee, Papa?"

"The man assured me a good placement in the inventor's competition. And he said that whatever I invent will earn me the money back, so I paid him 65 francs."

Belle began to grow weary of the day's surprises. She opened her mouth to reprimand her father, but quickly decided to keep quiet. How many times had she seen her father come home, tired from a long day's journey? How many nights had he fallen asleep before dinner was even served? Belle looked at Seymour and did not see a tired man who was beginning to despise his job. No, she saw a strong man whose passion was now reborn. *"We'll make things work."* She thought to herself.

Belle smiled again and grasped her papa's shoulders. After kissing him gently on his cheek, Belle stared into Seymour's eyes. "Papa, I will be honest; I cannot see much good in this situation right now, but to see you happy is all I can ask for in this world. In fact, I don't desire anything or anyone more than you and Lilly."

Seymour returned the embrace. "Not even Caspar?"

"What? Oh, Papa, no! At least, not right now! I barely know him. I don't even know if I can say that I love him."

"Is two years too short of time for you?"

"Remember, Papa, he only comes to visit twice a year for only a month. Therefore, I have only known him for a third of a year. We're practically strangers!"

"You know that, and I know that, but does Caspar?"

"I suppose not."

With a parting embrace, Belle went back inside the house, surprised to find that Lilly had return from the market. Belle gasped when she saw the state of being Lilly was in. Her hair was knotted and wild, her dress dirty and scandalously torn around the shoulder, and her face fiery pink and stained with tears. Belle was silent as she quickly grabbed a washcloth, but she did not hesitate to ask questions once she had approached her sister.

"I am sixteen, Belle," Lilly replied to Belle's interrogating. "Haven't I the right to keep some matters to myself?"

"I would assume so," Belle began cautiously. Handing her sister the damp cloth, she continued, "But something tells me that you don't want to keep this secret to yourself."

Lilly began to cry. "Some of the boys . . . in the village . . . decided they would have some fun and see how much roughhousing frail, little Lilly could take." Laughing a little, she added, "I think I did okay."

Belle smiled kindly, trying to hide her anger. Lilly had always been smaller than most girls her age, and some of the young adults in the village saw her has the perfect target for their pranks and jokes. Belle always tried to shelter her sister, but she knew that she could not protect Lilly forever and always. She needed a husband; she needed a strong man that would protect her from the bullies of the world. The only problem was that all the boys in the village, all the possible suitors, *were* the bullies.

"Who started the tussle?"

"His name is Jacob, the blacksmith's boy. If Caspar had not come along–"

"Caspar's back?" Belle interrupted. "He's the one who saved you?"

Lilly nodded. "I thought you'd be the first to know. But, yes, he was the one who stopped the tussle. He just shouted once, and Jacob seemed to fall right into line. Caspar came up and started to reprimand the boy in front of everyone! I thanked Caspar, and that's when I came home."

"Well, I am afraid that I don't have any good news for you either," Belle began.

"What do you mean?"

Belle sighed. "Lilly, Papa has quit his job. He's decided to become an inventor."

Lilly shook her head, but kept on smiling. "That's not too bad. I mean he could have chosen some more embarrassing professions."

"Oh yeah," Belle cried in mock offense, "Name a few."

Lilly rubbed her chin in thought. "Well there's, er . . . or what about . . . no, you know what's really embarrassing is . . . well to be honest, Belle, I can't think of any."

"I couldn't either."

"Oh, Belle, this could be bad! Everyone already thinks that our family is crazy; your infatuation with fairies, my weakness, and now Papa's desire to invent!"

Belle sat beside Lilly and rubbed her shoulders. "We can't let what others say define us, Lilly. If they think us mad, so what? We will hold our family name proudly, no matter what others think. Agreed?"

Lilly nodded. "Agreed."

Chapter Ten

Honesty Among Sisters

After a few minutes of asking around, Belle discovered that Caspar was located in the vacated tavern. She received directions from the baker's wife (who was well acquainted with every shop in the village), and quickly ran off to find her friend. Becoming timid upon arriving, Belle took a few steady breaths before she entered the tavern.

Finding herself in a dark and uncomfortably dusty room, Belle decided to leave the door open. Unfortunately, the sky was overcast, so there was not an ounce of sunlight to illuminate the cavernous place. Belle attempted to swat away the haze that lay before her eyes, but only stirred up more dust. Squinting, she saw a faint candle towards the back of the tavern. Belle relied on her hands to feel her way around as she cautiously made her way towards the flickering light.

As she neared the table, Belle yelped after being startled by the thudding noise of the front door. Now all light was gone, except for the little candle. Belle stood in the center of the room, torn by her fear of darkness and her persistence to find her friend. If she turned back, she would be outside again! But if she moved towards the candle, she would be able to take the light and search for Caspar. After deciding that she really wanted to see her friend, Belle gave herself an encouraging talk and walked towards the table.

Once she reached her destination, Belle saw a stout form slumped in the chair. The figure's back was towards her and his head rested on the table. Belle reached out and gently patted whom she assumed to be Caspar on the shoulder. However, her "How are you, Caspar?" was cut short by her own scream.

As soon as her hand brushed the young man, he fell straight to the floor as though he was dead! Feeling once again what she described as "the nausea of a fainting flower," Belle also crumpled to the floor. She began to shake and sob. Even in the poor light, she could see Caspar's face, frozen in painful agony. Belle cried out again.

"Belle?" A voice echoed from the darkness. The voice belonged to a man, and a drunken one at that. Belle looked up to see a form, stumbling around and lumbering towards her. Regaining her wits, she cried, "Who are you? What have you done with Caspar?"

The man laughed, which sounded more like a lazy gurgle. After tripping once or twice, the man took the dim candle and knelt before Belle. "You mean, 'What have I done to myself?'" The young man waved the candle dangerously close to his face.

"Oh Caspar!" Belle wept as she flung her arms around his neck. "I thought you were dead!" She buried her head into his shoulder as she sobbed; she was surprised to find that, where there was usually the brisk aroma of the outdoors, there was only the foul stench of alcohol. Belle held her breath and stayed close to her friend.

"Why would you think that?" Caspar slurred.

"They told me you were here and when I saw the body, I assumed this was you. Then I watched the body fall as soon as I touched . . . what *did* I touch?"

"The newest evidence of my hunting prowess." The young man swung his arm haphazardly towards the body. Belle sighed with relief when she only saw a bear. Reaching out, she brushed the animal's furry remains; just as she touched the skin, a blinding vision flashed before her eyes. A head, one belonging to a beast with monstrous features, was mounted on a wall. There was loud, rowdy laughter echoing everywhere. Men were gathered below the mount, warming themselves by a fire. They were all cheering and clapping, as if to praise a hero. Then a chant began, and like one thunderous drum, the name Caspar was pounded into the air. Belle drew in a breath to scream, but the vision left quicker than it came. Turning back to Caspar, Belle pleaded for fresh air and sunlight.

Once outside, the two sat on the front steps of the tavern. Putting her vision aside, Belle turned her attention to Caspar. She was truly happy to see him again, but his present state of being frightened her; Belle had never seen Caspar drunk, nor had she ever seen his countenance so depressed. Politely clearing her throat, Belle asked, "Why are you like this, Caspar?"

"I am reveling in a celebratory toast! Besides, is that not what tavern men do? Buy a few rounds, make some speeches?"

"I've heard that they don't normally drink alone. I believe there is more than that, though. Why are you here?"

"I'm here because I tought the bavern, er, bought the tavern."

"Why?"

"Because this," Caspar raised his voice as he jerked his entire arm back towards the tavern, "Was my brother's dream! I did this to honor him. The brandy just helps me to bear the pain of loss."

Belle rested her hand on Caspar's shoulder. "How long has he, your brother, been gone?"

"Four years last night, he was 'possed to come home. But did he?" Caspar flung his head from side to side. "My parents and I waited up all night, and we stayed up the next night, too. We waited for nearly a week with no word. After a month, my parents decided to accept the truth: their eldest son was dead!"

Caspar buried his face in his hands, crying softly as he continued the story. "He . . . had been called to battle; I assume that's where he died. The only promise that my brother ever broke was his promise to return after the battle was won. You would have loved my brother, Belle. He had the gracefulness of my French mother, and he 'ad the rugged looks of m' Italian father. He was a real man."

The young man kept on talking and babbling, but he made less sense with every word. Belle wrapped her arms around his shoulders and helped him to stand up. After deciding he should not go home (he needed sleep, not a lecture from his aunt), Belle helped Caspar to her house. Fearing that she could never lift him if he lay down, Belle propped Caspar against the side of the house while she opened the door to the workshop cellar. Belle wrapped Caspar's arm around her shoulder and began to descend the steps, stumbling all the way. With Caspar still leaning against her, Belle pulled some of the hay bales from the wall, hoping to create a makeshift bed.

"Thankyou," Caspar mumbled as Belle laid him down on the hay.

"You're welcome," Belle whispered as she pulled a blanket over Caspar. "Try not to toss and turn," she commented in a motherly voice.

Taking her hand like he did in the bookstore, Caspar tried to plant a kiss upon her knuckles, but ended up blowing his affection into the air. Belle shook her head in pity and amusement. After patting him gently on his cheek, Belle said farewell and ascended to the surface. When she reached the top step, she was surprised to see a face looking her way. "Oh, Lilly! I didn't know you were home."

"I just came back," she lied. Lilly was still at quarrels with herself about whether or not to tell Belle about *her* feelings for Caspar. After watching this new interaction, however, she could not help but feel that maybe Belle was a better match for the man. But Lilly was still gnawed by the feeling of guilt; she had never kept a secret from Belle, and yet here she was, lying to protect her own feelings.

"Walk with me?" Belle nodded her head towards the adjacent fields and forest. Linking arm in arm, the two sisters wandered aimlessly, happy just to be together. After embracing a few moments of silence, Belle asked, "What if our lives were like fairy tales?"

Lilly carefully considered her answer. "Honestly, Belle, I don't think I would like living in a fairy tale."

Neither of them said anything else for a while. Belle and Lilly continued to drift through the fields, until they found a perfect clearing, a place where the tall grass had been trod down and a solitary tree offered shade. After discussing the weather, the day in general, and their father's new hobby that he called his job, Belle turned back to their earlier conversation. "Why wouldn't you enjoy living in a fairy tale, Lilly? You would be a princess! Knights and princes would clamor to win your heart. Adventure, romance, and a happily ever after would all be yours. Why wouldn't you want that?"

Lilly sighed. At times like this, she always remembered that Belle had another family, another history, and another *life* before she came to them. If she wanted the life of a fantasy princess, Lilly would voice no objections; but a fairy tale life had nothing to offer, in her opinion. Casually shrugging, Lilly answered, "I guess I don't care for that kind of stuff. I am a background girl, Belle, not a princess. If our lives were to be shoved into a book, honestly I would rather just be left out.

"I would rather live out my days as a simple girl, knowing that someone is not reading about me, forming his or her own opinions about who I am. Moreover, as far as *adventure* is concerned, it can just stay home and not come calling on me! I do not want the romance of a princess with knights and princes begging to marry her. I want one man who truly loves me for who I am, not for a royal title. And I won't ask for a happily ever after, because I don't believe they exist."

Belle, who had followed her sister's conversation in silence, cocked her head and stared in disbelief. "No happy endings? Lilly, surely you don't believe that!"

In a hushed tone, Lilly replied, "I most certainly do. We will not have a 'happily ever after' until we go to Heaven. Here, in this life, there are always going to be days where there are few praiseworthy things. I do not mean to sound so dismal, Belle. This is just something I believe."

"You could never sound dismal, Lilly. I always hear the silver linings somewhere behind your words. You are entitled to believe what you want, no matter how strange your beliefs might sound to other people. You do bring up some very interesting ideas, and I thank you for sharing with me. I appreciate your honesty."

"Time for no more secrets." Lilly cleared her throat. Raising her arm slightly, she began to twirl and twist the ends of her hair. "Belle, what are your feelings for Caspar?"

Belle opened her mouth and quickly found out that she had nothing to say. Lilly never talked about Caspar, at least not on such a personal level. Not knowing the full extent of Lilly's own feelings, Belle decided to proceed cautiously. "Lilly, if you are asking me if I love him, I will have to give you an affirmative no."

"What? I thought, ever since the day in the bookstore, you loved him."

Belle went on to explain that she had come close to loving Caspar, but after watching his behavior, she realized she could never love him unless he matured. "There are some things in Caspar's life that needed to change, not for my personal benefit, but for his. He can be self-centered and egotistical some times; I think Caspar puffs himself up because he doubts the man he is.

"In addition, as I have just recently witnessed, he can make wrong decisions in times of grief. He grieves because he was hurt in the past. I think that, if he does not healthfully let go of the past, the pain and wrong decisions are only going to get worse. And for being eighteen, almost a man, he can be very childish at times."

Lilly stood and squared her shoulders. Her heart soared at the thought of being freed from a two-year secret. "Belle," she spoke confidently, "I love him. And I know you might not approve –"

"I do and don't."

"... Even though he has faults, I love him. And I understand that you are hurt –"

"I'm not."

"But I didn't know how you felt towards Caspar. I didn't want to break your heart –"

"You wouldn't have."

"... If you did love him. And ... wait, what have you been saying?"

Belle stood and joined her sister. "Well first of all, I said that I do and don't approve. I do approve, because I think Caspar would protect you and care for you; I do not quite approve yet, because there are many things Caspar must learn before he becomes a suitable husband. Second, I said I am not angry. Third, I said you wouldn't have broken my heart." Belle pulled Lilly close to her. "My heart can never be broken by your honesty, Lilly. I will always want you to tell me the truth!"

They walked back to the house together, reveling in the time that they had shared. Before they reached the house, Lilly asked Belle another question of great importance to her.

"Why is Caspar the way he is today?"

"He's mourning his brother who was killed. Four years ago last night, I believe."

"That's interesting."

Belle stopped and turned. "Don't you think that's a little morbid to describe a death as 'interesting?'"

"That's not what I meant. I was referencing the coincidence. Four years ago last night, you went out to play in the woods. But you did not come back, not even when we called for you. Papa went out and searched the whole woods; the next morning, he found you in a hole. Do you remember that?"

Belle nodded. She remembered being lifted from the ground and then coming home. But when she tried to remember instances before that, her mind went blank. Belle had only feelings, no solid memories, but she did not have the feeling of having fun or playing. Fear, a desire for survival, and loneliness were the only feelings she recalled when she tried to mentally recreate that time. If Lilly was correct, she should have been having a fun time in the woods and then she fell in the hole by mistake. However, Belle had a nagging feeling that she was *placed* in the hole, and she was agitated because she could not remember why or by whom. Shrugging off the past once again, Belle continued her walk with Lilly in silence.

Lilly bit her tongue. She had been eaten up on the inside by guilt for not telling Belle about something as trivial as her feelings for Caspar, yet here she was telling an even greater lie. Her conscience felt pulled in multiple directions. Lilly wanted Belle to know the truth, she really did, but what damage might the truth inflict? Belle would certainly be crushed and possibly want to move away, leaving Seymour and Lilly without someone whom they both loved very much. As they neared the house, Lilly resolved to stay silent. She did not want to lose the sister she always wanted.

Chapter Eleven

Accusations, Rejections, and Expeditions

"Witch!"

"Corrupter!"

"Leave our village; you don't belong here anymore!"

Belle huddled against her bedroom wall, wishing that the window would completely block out the accusing cries of the crowd. She started to cry, praying that the people would leave and forget their anger. For hours, they had stood by her house, yelling threats and accusations. Some had even been daring enough to light torches and brandish pitchforks. Rocks thudded against the walls and rotten fruit splattered on the windows. The screams never stopped.

Belle's ears throbbed from the noise and her eyes stung from the tears. What had *she* done to deserve their hate? Belle had lived in this town all her life; why, after seventeen years, why were the people turning on her now? After drawing her knees up to her chest and wrapping her arms around her legs, Belle began to rock herself in consolation.

What had she done?

Three Days Ago

Madam Louise Chantelle stood in the shadows of the dressmaker's doorway as she watched Mademoiselle Belle walk down the street. She was trying to grow accustomed to the girl while, at the same time, treating Belle as if she had always been a part of the Dubois family. But Louise was bothered by the girl's peculiar obsession with books and fairies. Louise would admit that she too, in her youth, tried to believe in magical creatures, but she tossed her childish imaginations aside as soon as she entered womanhood. *"Belle should learn to do the same if she ever wants the chance to marry my nephew!"*

"You don't care much for that Dubois girl, do you?" Alice, the dressmaker's wife, had been observing Madam Chantelle, and, after seeing the scorn on her face, decided this would be a perfect time to scoop up some delicious gossip.

"It's not that I don't *like* Belle; I just think that her flighty imaginations and fantasies might be contagious to the children of this village. *Our* children. The children that we are trying so hard to train in upright and sensible ways."

"I agree," cried Alice. "Yesterday, my son Andrew came home as giddy as a toddler, claiming that Belle had taught him a story of a thief, a large vine, and angered giant! I have a feeling that soon all our children will be poisoned by Belle's fairy tale lies."

"What a most distressing thought! Now I will admit that my husband is partly to blame. If he had only kept logical books in his library, there would be no fairy tale book from which Belle could teach!"

"Well, while I think the book helped her obsession, I don't believe that it started Belle's infatuations with the fairy people. I have heard that she showed a firm belief in these creatures long before she read the book." (Even though this statement of Belle was true, Alice had *not* heard the fact, but just assumed the truth.)

"Alice, dear, one thing I know to be true is this: only witches, sorcerers, unwise children, and adults who are not mentally sound believe in fairies. I believe Belle is becoming dangerous to our society."

And so the women prattled on, unaware of the dangerous flame that they were so passionately fanning.

"Belle? Please, let me in. Everyone is gone. You're safe." Caspar stood patiently on the Dubois' porch, hoping Belle would not be afraid to open the door.

There was a patter of feet and then a slow groan of the floor. Caspar smiled as the door began to open, but sighed when he realized that Belle was only going to open the door a crack and no more. Feeling playful and mischievous, Caspar leaned his head a peeked through the crack, which was like a sliver of shadow that was blocking him and the outside world from entering the house. But even in the shadow, Caspar could still see half of Belle's face, pale and frightened. Her gorgeously soft brown eyes were glazed by past floods of tears, and they searched frantically for any approaching evil. Smiling compassionately, Caspar put his hand around the edge of the door. "Why don't we go for a walk? You could use the fresh air."

Belle reluctantly nodded and proceeded through the door and into the consoling embrace of a friend. She was embarrassed when she realized that there was one of Caspar's friends standing a next to them. "Who is this, Caspar?"

"Ah. This is my cousin, Louis Alexandre. He was in the village to visit Uncle Cartier, so I asked him to come along to . . . to –"

"To chaperone our walk together?" Both Caspar and Louis nodded vigorously. Belle turned and shook Louis' hand. "Thank for being willing to do so, sir. I know Papa would be honored to know that I was chaperoned while he was away. Also, thank you, Caspar, for coming to get me. I was frightened about being alone in the house, not knowing if that crowd was going to come back or not, more vicious than before."

"Where is your father? And Lilly?"

Belle shrugged. "I don't know exactly where, but they went to retrieve some supplies for Papa's inventions." Belle gave a detailed report of all her father's work, every eccentric toy and invention he had created, but Caspar could tell by her monotone voice that she did not really feel like talking about her father.

"What's really on your mind, Belle?"

Belle stopped walking and stared intensely at Caspar, warning him to tell the truth. "What have I done wrong, Caspar?"

Caspar kept quiet for such a long while, looking at the distant horizon, that Belle began to wonder if he would even answer her at all. Actually, he was thinking of how to easily tell her that he knew exactly why some of the village people had turned against her; Caspar had overheard a conversation between his aunt and uncle. He grimaced when he recalled Aunt Louise's incriminating accusations. And even though Caspar found himself partially agreeing with his aunt, he could not bring himself to view Belle as a witch or a danger to society.

"Well that's an easy question to answer," Louis giggled. "They think you're a luna–" Caspar quickly wrapped his hand over his cousin's mouth. He knew what his cousin was going to say, and he did not dare let Belle hear the word *lunatic*. Even though there was some truth in what Louis almost said, Caspar knew that the moment would be ruined if Belle thought the people deemed her mad.

"Pardon?"

Caspar sighed; he knew that what Belle needed to hear and what he wanted to tell her were quite different. "The villagers are apprehensive about your beliefs, specifically, your adoration for fairy tales and the like, and your faith in the existence of fairies themselves. They are afraid that you are poisoning the minds of the children."

"Poisoning?!" Belle stepped back. "Do you agree with them?"

"No, of course not." Caspar's stomach sank, knowing that he had just lied to his love, but he reassured his conscience that he could not tell her the truth. Caspar nodded towards Louis, who quickly and quietly turned and added some distance between Caspar and himself. Drawing closer to Belle, Caspar continued, "Belle, I love you, and no gossip could ever change my feelings for you! I wanted to get you out of your house so you could escape from the madness, but I think I should now admit my ulterior motive. Belle, I have known you for a little over three years now, and, if I may be honest, I loved you when I first met you."

"*No!*" Belle's heart screamed in fear.

"And so, I want to ask if you would consider being my wife?" As he spoke, Caspar knelt down and pulled a ring from his jacket pocket.

Belle started to cry, which made Caspar smile, thinking that he had overwhelmed his "fiancée" with joy. In harsh reality, Belle was crying because she knew that whichever answer she gave, at least two hearts would be broken. If she said yes, she would break Lilly's heart. If she said no, Caspar's heart would be the one to shatter. In any case, her heart would most definitely crack a little. Pulling Caspar off his bended knee, Belle told him as kindly as she could, "I can't marry you, Caspar."

"Why not?"

The air was so thick and silent that Belle could have sworn that she heard the sound of Caspar's fracturing heart. Meanwhile, she felt her own heart sink a meter or two. "I can't . . . because –"

Caspar gripped Belle's shoulders tightly, shaking her slightly. "Is there someone else? Someone who could provide for you better than I could? Someone who could love you more passionately than I love you now? Who, Belle? Who?"

Belle writhed and squirmed, but she kept her gaze steady; she wanted Caspar to know that she was being honest, and that she could not be bullied into marrying anyone. A moment ago she had been sorry that she might have hurt the man's heart, but now she felt like spitting in his face. The rage that burned in Caspar's eyes and the hateful sneer that contorted his face were both glimmers of who Caspar really was. He had no conceivable idea of how to treat a lady, even if the lady had just refused his proposal. Pushing herself out of Caspar's grip, she stood boldly and told Caspar the truth.

"There *is* no one else, you chauvinist pig! You think that every woman is inferior to you, and because of their lesser position, they dreamily look up to you! You think that every lady of marrying age should just fall for you, easy and simple! Well let me tell you this: you are my friend, though your current actions have shown me a new side of you that I am almost glad I have seen, but I do not love you, Caspar!"

Tears began to burn Belle's eyes for the fifth time that day. Belle looked away, becoming strangely fascinated with the ground below her. She looked back at Caspar, still expecting to see his anger raging. Instead, she saw a broken man, a man that was just as hurt as she was, and a man that was already internally reprimanding himself for losing his temper.

"Won't you reconsider?" Caspar was pleading, something Belle had never heard him do before.

Belle shook her head, her soft curls dancing as she did so. "I am sorry, Caspar. I deeply care for you as my friend, but I can't imagine my feelings ever becoming anything more intimate." Belle paused and took a step closer, reaching for Caspar's shoulder. "There *is* someone else who does love you more than –"

Caspar brushed her away. "Forgive me, Belle, for sounding selfish, but there is no one else I could ever want. Forgive me for putting you in the awkward situation and for losing my temper. I guess my heart has not learned a gentlemanly way of dealing with pain and rejection." Hanging his head, Caspar turned and started to walk away. Stopping after a few paces, Caspar called over his shoulder, "I do want our friendship to continue, but I think that we should spend some time apart."

Belle nodded and turned away. Taking deep breaths, both friends started walking away from one path of life and moved on to another. With each step the distance grew, the friendship waned, the pain strengthened, and the heartstrings bitterly frayed. Caspar rejoined his cousin and went to the tavern to douse his pain with the soothing intoxication of a drink once again; there he sat for hours, each sip soaking his heart in a new wave of hatred and animosity.

Belle, however, decided to choose a better way. Half way home, she realized that, if she did go into her house, the lonely atmosphere would perfectly cultivate her sulky mood. Belle pictured herself, sitting alone, freely allowing guilt and pity to overwhelm her. Why could she not go out on an adventure instead?

Running to the house, Belle made up her mind to go traveling through the woods. Seymour and Lilly were not to be back for a few days, giving her plenty of time to explore, and possibly spend the night under the stars. She grabbed a few blankets, her shawl, a book, and a few other necessities. After packing food in her old leather satchel and writing a quick note explaining her whereabouts (in case her family arrived before she did), Belle headed to the barn.

Seymour had taken Pierre, the young colt he had bought a few months ago; when Seymour found out that the occupation of an inventor did require a little traveling, he graciously put Philippe into retirement. Philippe, however, still enjoyed traveling, even though Seymour refused to force an older horse to travel such long distances. *"A short trip in the woods will be good for Philippe,"* Belle thought. *"The exercise will do him good! And to see that he is still needed might help him overcome his apparent jealousy for Pierre."*

The trip was indeed good for Philippe, in both physical and mental states. Belle smiled when she saw how happy her horse became when she reached for his all-but-torn saddle, which looked pitifully neglected. The old horse nearly bolted from his stable, youthfully rejuvenated by the thought of being wanted again. Philippe whinnied and shook his head while Belle tightened the straps of the saddle. Mounting with grace and ease, Belle prodded Philippe into a light walk.

As they headed into the neighboring forest and woods, Belle breathed in the fresh air. This was what she needed to recalibrate, to let the pains of the afternoon roll away. Her senses tingled, stimulated by the sounds and smells of the forest. She looked up and admired the crisp sky that hid behind the canopy of spindly, nearly bare branches of the trees. The damp leaves and fallen twigs muffled the strong clip-clops of Philippe's mighty hoofs.

Everywhere Belle looked, she was greeted by the brilliant colors of autumn. Some leaves fought to stay green and bright, not yet willing to accept the coming of winter. They were, however, a minority. All trees wore the Robes of Fall; their branches were graced with rusts and oranges, yellows and reds. Through the leaves blew a lively wind, calling to all who would dare explore the daunting forest.

Belle ventured until sunset, going deeper into the woods and never turning back. After finding a sufficiently cleared piece of ground, Belle spread out the blankets and prepared herself for sleep. She loosely tied Philippe to a nearby tree trunk, wishing that the horse could roam free; Belle knew that Philippe would never purposely leave her, but strange and unfamiliar noises could easily send any horse to flight.

Tossing away the day's worries and traumas, Belle laid down onto her self-made cot. The last thing she saw was the dim, amber glow of the sun on her right, and the silken chill of the moon on her left. Belle thought about herself as she closed her eyes for the final time. She was sleeping alone in the woods, with no means of protection and no roaring fire, and yet she felt no fear. Why was she not nervous or curious about the dangers that lurked in the shadows? Belle's parting thought consoled her as she drifted to sleep: *"I have a connection to these woods. I feel safe. I am supposed to be here."*

Chapter Twelve

A Castle Found

Belle did sleep under the stars, and she did so quite peaceably. As special as her night was, the morning was even more magical. Chickadees and blue jays sang and the wind whistled, telling Belle that now was the perfect time to wake. Hearing their cries, Belle stretched and yawned, rejoicing that a new day had come. She looked around, her eyes adjusting to the rays of sunlight. As sleep left her, so did Belle's painful memories of yesterday. Today was a brand new day!

"Something thrilling is going to happen today, Philippe. I can feel the excitement in the air!"

After Belle packed up her campsite, ate a small meal, and performed Philippe's daily grooming ritual, she considered turning back for home. Philippe seemed to think that returning home was the right idea. He whinnied and brayed, walked towards his saddle, and nudged the reigns and bridle. Belle smiled, glad to see that there were still some sparks left in the old horse. Walking to him, Belle rested her head gently on Philippe's neck and lovingly brushed his face.

"I wouldn't mind going home myself, Philippe; but I would only return if I knew there was someone there to greet me. I can't stay in that place by myself anymore, for I would live in constant fear that the people might return to do me harm." She paused, glancing in the direction of home. "Then again, I wouldn't want to stay out here any longer if Papa and Lilly are there, waiting for my return."

Belle realized that she was most likely in hearing distance from her house. Stepping away from Philippe, Belle inhaled deeply and shouted for her father. There was no response. Belle, deciding once again to disturb the morning silence, repeated the process and called again, this time shouting Lilly's name. Again, there was no answer. Belle mounted Philippe and road him on the opposite direction from whence she came. She was satisfied that no answer meant no one was home, and that she could continue her adventure in the woods.

Philippe and Belle, partners in the expedition, traveled up, down, and through the woods until midday. When the sun was high and the shadows had vanished, Belle decided to take a break from her exploration. They stopped at a stream, for which the extremely thirsty horse was grateful, and stayed there for a short while. As Belle sat on a rock by the bank, she became mesmerized by the steady flow of the river. She was lulled into a peaceful state by the babbling cries of the water and by the golden glints of the sun's reflections. Belle laughed as she watched her horse playfully trot into the middle of the water, cooling his hooves and satisfying his thirst.

"Philippe," Belle began, feeling no shame in freely talking to her horse, "We have traveled nearly half this forest, wouldn't you say? I *have* had fun, but I feel like we have wandered aimlessly and without purpose. Well, I have thought of something we should do: follow this river to the beginning!"

Philippe turned his head toward Belle, and then looked back towards the water, seemingly uninterested in the current conversation. He shook his mane and stomped his foot in protest of anymore traveling, except for the journey home.

"I have a vague memory of this river," Belle continued. "I remember being drawn here by sounds: sounds of fairies! I remember a feeling of sadness and disappointment." Belle's eyes slowly filled with tears. "I want to leave this river too, Philippe; I want to leave this river in my past, locked away as a soon-to-be forgotten memory. I feel like I need to see where this river leads. Will you help me see this last venture out, my friend?" Belle asked.

Philippe trotted out of the river, splashing the water and sploshing the mud. Stopping by Belle, the horse shook his neck and tail, reluctantly agreeing to continue the journey. Belle gave Philippe a thank-you pat and mounted her horse.

Therefore, the friends continued on, searching for the river's start. "Just imagine, Philippe," Belle's voice was filled with child-like awe, "Just imagine what this riverhead will be like. I think there will be a small mountain that is just as majestic as the more grandeur mountains. There will be snow, tons of snow that gently covers the mountain's peaks. And when the snow begins to melt, water trickles down the mountainside, running down into this valley to form this river."

Unfortunately, the riverhead was not what was what Belle had hoped to see. The young woman had become so focused on the river, constantly watching the rippling water slowly move onwards, that she had lost focus of her surroundings. Bright autumn trees were now sparse; only bare, gray trees were seen. Even though not much time had lapsed forward, this part of the forest was dark and bleak. Shadows danced and played about as if the sun had already set.

Belle noticed that the river was narrowing into a stream. She prodded Philippe forward, eager to reach her journey's end. Navigating their way through a grove of bushes and brambles, they discovered that the riverhead was nothing more than an elevated pond. Hearing the sound of water dripping into water, Belle nudged Philippe forward again, hoping to discover a serene waterfall or angelic fountain.

But all that was found was a wall, on which sat a disfigured statue of a gargoyle. The statue's shoulders hunched forward, and the wings were spread out, as if the monster was ready to take flight. Even though no fangs were shown (the gargoyle's stony lips were pursed into a tiny circle), the hideous scowl on the monster's face was much more frightening than any teeth could ever be. Cold, murky water spewed from the statue's mouth, and fell into the pond below. Though the pond branched out into another river that twisted to the right side of the castle, neither horse nor girl felt like exploring anymore.

Belle's stomach clenched and her hand flew up to her mouth. Here was the riverhead that she had hoped to discover, but she now wished that she had never set out on this journey. Belle could not help but think of how the river she had come to admire, the river that she had just *drank* from, was nothing more than a gargoyle's vomitus projectiles. The disgusting thought plagued her mind for a while. Pulling the reigns to the left, Belle led Philippe and herself away from the frightening wall. However, after a few minutes of traveling, Belle discovered that the wall was actually a part of a castle. An *old* castle.

"Philippe, could I convince you to join me for *one* more adventure? Let's find the gate to this castle, peek in, and then go back home." Without waiting for any telltale signs of a response, Belle continued the exploration. There was indeed a gate, and it was built of wrought iron with veins of gold. There was nothing in the courtyard except for a few withered trees and some bristly bushes. Everything was gray and cold, just like the castle's surroundings. Belle dismounted her horse and cautiously walked up to the gate.

"Hello?" No response. The only reply that Belle heard was her own voice echoing across the court and the lonely howl of the wind. *"Must be abandoned."* But no sooner had Belle thought this thought to herself, she saw a faint flicker of light, candle light, coming from a distant window of the castle.

Belle felt as though she should return to Philippe and ride home, but as she continued to stare at the castle gate, she knew that she had seen this place before. *"Perhaps in a dream"* Belle thought, *"Or a vision!"* Suddenly, the memory became clear. Belle, on the night that the Chantelles had come over for dinner, had seen this same castle in her brief, frightening vision. Never before had Belle felt so led to enter a stranger's abode, but something called her, beckoned her, to open the gate and slowly walk through the courtyard.

Philippe nickered and the gate crashed shut. Belle quickly turned around to see that she was now locked inside an eerie castle without her friend. Frightened, Philippe lost his sense of loyalty and ran back into the woods. He would rather face the darkness than the unknown dangers of the castle. Belle attempted to call him back, but her horse was already too far away. She would have to find another way out.

Turning back around, Belle took a few more paces forward. *"In a place like this, I should feel fear, right?"* But Belle could not help but smile. She was on her own, free to explore and look around this castle. She had no sheltering father to warn her of uncertain dangers, no motherly sister to tell her that adventure was overrated, and no nagging horse telling her to go home! Even though she loved each member of her family, Belle's heart soared with the thought of her freedom.

Belle gleefully ran across the paved stones, leaving all her hesitations at the gate. She first came to a door, which was comfortingly similar to the door of the bookstore. The door was carved from oak and was beautifully weathered. There were a few long gashes running down the front, causing sharp splinters to jut out of the door. Now a normal person would have gently opened the front door and started their exploration from there. But Belle, being far from normal, decided to leave the front door and find a back entrance into the castle.

As she began to walk around the castle, Belle found a garden, which she believed to be a once-beautiful place. Belle strolled around, searching hopefully for the faintest scent of a flower. As Belle traveled about in the garden, gently petting the barren hedges, she struggled to find any signs of life, that is, until she heard a faint song echoing through the garden. Belle continued on, searching desperately for the singer, trying use her sense of hearing as a guide.

The maiden stopped halfway to her destination. She had only heard a melody, but now she heard the words. Belle stopped, trying not to stagger or crumple; the words touched her heart in such a way that tears were inevitable. The song was sung by a boy, a lonely boy, asking *why* he was alone. The boy continued to sing his song of questions, asking his enemy to come back to him and to be his friend again, wondering why his friend had even become his enemy, asking what he himself had done wrong.

Belle's heart ached for this boy. Adding speed to her pace, Belle ran around the final hedge, ready to draw this boy close to her. The motherly spirit in her heart wanted embrace this boy, tell him everything was going to be all right, and that he was never really alone. But deciding that her sudden presence might startle the child, Belle slowed and walked around the corner slowly.

There she saw him, her singing boy. However, since there was barely any light in the sky, Belle could not see him well. All she could see was a small boy, sitting on the ground. His back was slightly bent and his head drooped. There were a few figurines lying about his feet, sadly tossed away by a despondent child. Belle was disappointed to hear that the music had stopped, but she understood that a heavy heart does not always want to sing.

"Don't stop," Belle cooed. She slowly began to approach the boy, her footsteps crunching the abnormally dead grass beneath her feet. "I did enjoy your song." Belle could not imagine the pain the child's heart must have felt; the boy still sat, not even moving to address Belle. Feeling motherly, Belle knelt down and gently rested her hand on the boy's shoulders. The boy still did not react. He did not even flinch. *"Maybe he just needs to see my face."* Using the boy's shoulders as a pivot point, Belle swung her body around in front of the boy.

Here is where Belle discovered something terrifying: they boy had not moved or said anything because he was a statue! Belle's breath froze as she surveyed the realism and surreal details of the statue. Each strand of hair, each wrinkle of fabric, and each complex emotion seemed to be individually carved by a perfectionist. Cupping her hands around the boy's face, Belle felt minute bumps sporadically placed on the boy's pronounced cheeks. Belle realized that the little bulges were tears, never to complete their stony descent.

But what of the song? Belle swore to herself that she had indeed heard music, but where was the singer? Obviously, the statue was not the one to sing; that would go against all the logical laws of nature and science. The young woman decided to explore more of the garden, hoping to find her real mystery singer.

After another half hour of searching, Belle returned to the statue, still having found no living person in the area. Belle sat down in front of the boy again and stared intently at his face; his mouth hung slightly open as though he wanted to tell her a story, but he could not begin to find the words. Belle sighed and leaned her head against the statue's forehead.

Instantaneously, Belle received another vision. The statue slowly began to rise and walk backwards as if his life was being rewound. Stone and marble slowly melted away into skin, and chips of granite gradually became strands of silky hair. After a few moments of being gone, the boy came back, walking in a normal fashion this time.

As he sat down and began to sing, Belle physically saw the song being turned into what appeared to be rippling, translucent waves. These waves floated around the boy and around the garden, soaking into all the bushes, trees, and rocks. As the vision faded, Belle heard the words, "Matter has memory; we remember everything."

Back in the present, Belle heard a faint hum begin to rise from the ground. Soon a myriad of voices joined the hum, forming a beautiful, invisible choir. The bushes' leaves began to resonate, sending forth the melody. The branches shook, echoing the words to the song. When the ground started thumping out a rhythm, Belle leapt to her feet, amazed and confused. Everything around her was singing the boy's song!

"How is this possible?" Belle cried out, afraid that she had fallen into a bewitched place. Then she remembered her vision. "Matter has memory," were the words she had heard; could that possibly be the answer to the phenomenon she was now experiencing?

Belle began to pace, playing out all scenarios in her head. What if there was a real boy? A boy who would come into this garden to sing, and have his song unknowingly soaked up by his surroundings? When the boy could not come anymore, perhaps due to illness or death, the garden inhabitants wanted to fill the empty space in the garden by remembering the boy's song, by making the music he had sung to them so many times. Feeling brave, and slightly silly, Belle tried talking to her surroundings. "Is that what happened?" She asked. "You sing now because you miss him?"

The music stopped, causing Belle to wander if she had imagined everything. But soon a new sound rose, and Belle thought she heard a voice trying to speak to her. "*Yes*," the voice replied.

"Is the voice I am hearing comprised of the garden inhabitants? The bushes, trees, and such?"

"*Yes.*"

Pointing to the statue, Belle inquired, "Is this a statute of the boy who would sing to you?"

"*Yes.*"

"What is his name?"

"*Timothy.*"

Belle decided to ask a daring question. "Would I be wise if I decided to explore the rest of this castle?"

"*No.*"

Belle was shocked to finally receive a negative response. Feeling indignant, Belle required the garden to tell her why she should not explore. There was no response for a long while, except for a rustling noise, which Belle assumed was the sound bushes make when they are conferring with one another and with their friends. Soon, everyone replied in unison.

"*Beast!*"

Chapter Thirteen
Loathing at First Sight

Adam was well familiar with each scent in the castle, even though every aroma muddled together in a dank, musty stench. This scent was different, one he had not smelled in what felt like an extremely long while: he smelled a human. The scent both pleased and frightened his animal instinct. Adam shook himself. "Have I changed so much that human flesh smells foreign to me now?" Even though he tried to convince himself that he had only been a monster a few months, Adam could not deny that four years had indeed passed. Four lonely, tortuous years.

Nose to the ground, Adam galloped through the palace. Adam was upset that another human had been able to easily enter his castle, yet he held on to the hope that this intruder was perhaps Sabella Rose. Adam had spent so many nights dreaming of this prophesied girl, the one who would come to judge his changed heart and grant him a reformed body.

In his dreams, Adam imagined what Sabella would look like; she would be most beautiful, an embodiment of royalty and grace. A thin, silver crown would rest upon her head, her golden locks flowing out beneath. Her piercing blue eyes were illuminated with love and forgiveness. In every dream, Adam saw Sabella standing before him, regal as a princess, with a rose delicately clasped between her hands.

Finally, Adam found his quarry. She had just entered from the garden; Adam could smell the fresh air on her clothes and in her hair. After having been locked away in the dark castle for nearly half a decade, the monster could see as well as any owl. After quietly approaching, Adam saw the stranger clearly, and he began to growl with disappointment and disgust. The girl's hair was disheveled, stringy, and unprofessionally groomed. Her dress was slightly frayed around the hem and sprinkled with dust. *"She might be a pretty peasant,"* Adam thought to himself. *"But she is a peasant nonetheless."*

"Hello?" The woman's voice was pleasant, but the word dripped with fear. Adam chuckled. He found the manner in which the girl called out to be humorous; she called to someone distant, completely unaware of his lumbering presence. Drawing deeper into the shadows, Adam thought he would have a little fun with the girl, playing on her emotions to entertain himself. After all, four years with no fun can make a monster extremely dull.

Belle found the inside of the castle more disturbing than the exterior. The room she was in was cold and dark, and had all the charm of a mortuary. There were no candles, causing Belle to squint and strain her eyes. Unfortunately, she could only see the faintest of details. She started walking, expecting to trip over a myriad of old furniture, yet her walk went smoothly enough. There was nothing in the room to give the impression of an inhabitant, but Belle held on to the hope that there was someone there to welcome to her.

"Hello?" The only answer was Belle's own voice, echoing off the cold walls.

After a few minutes of complete silence, Belle heard a sound that would have caused any other person to run away. But Belle decided to stay, partly because of brave curiosity, partly because her legs were frozen in traumatizing fear. The sound was comparable to the sound of iron nails being scraped across stone; so long and drawn out this sound was that Belle began to cringe. Her ears screamed in protest to the horrible, poisonous, and high-pitched scraping.

Then everything stopped. Time stood still and so did Belle. She tried to control her breathing, so as not to let whatever was out there know she was petrified. Belle's shoulders and arms were willing to move, trembling violently before whatever presence surrounded them, but her legs would not comply with any sort of mental or verbal command. Belle stiffened; something had approached her from behind. Soon a hot, sticky breath heated up her back. Belle cringed again, feeling as though Death himself was breathing upon her.

Hoping to take the creature by surprise, Belle flung her hand backward. She screamed as her wrist made contact with a protruding cheekbone. Belle attempted to pull her hand back to her side, but discovered that her slender fingers had become tangled in a mass of oily hair. She shrieked as she felt gnats and little crumbs roll down her arm. The creature only grunted. Belle was sure that this was her end; the monster would start by snapping off her hand, then possibly her head.

But everything turned out differently than Belle imagined. Large, muscular hands slowly wrapped around Belle's fingers, setting them free from their hairy trap. "There was no need for that," the creature growled as he referred to Belle's furious slap. Even though the voice was perturbed, Belle sensed the creature was attempting to speak kindly.

"I was frightened," Belle was surprised that she was able to respond with ease.

"I . . . apologize." Adam was shocked that he had even been able to say those two words.

"And there was no need to scare me like you did. I did not come here to hurt you."

The Beast told Adam not to trust this girl. Who was she to come into their castle and lie about her intentions? She was here to hurt or even kill them! *"Peasants are selfish,"* the Beast thought, *"She has probably come to turn us into food for her savage village."* But for once, Adam refused to believe the Beast. As he walked back into the shadows, he said, "I was expecting someone else. When I saw that you were not her –"

"I apologize for not being the girl whom you expect," Belle interrupted, her fear replaced by a slight fiery tone of voice. "But you should treat your guests more properly." Belle squinted, hoping to see the man she was talking to, and perhaps see what he looked like. "Just because I am myself and not someone else does not give you the right to treat me as your next meal!"

"I hold all the rights in this castle!" The monster screamed in acrimony. "This is my castle, and you are nothing but an obtrusive commoner!" Adam bit his tongue. He knew that the girl would run away now, abhorred by Adam's rage, but he almost yearned for her to stay. Adam could not deny that he was lonely and desired company. He contemplated apologizing and asking for the woman to stay, but the Beast reminded Adam that he had already apologized and that was enough for one day.

Yet, the woman stayed, and better still, she did not raise her temper in return. She smiled compassionately, but Adam saw the heartache in her eyes. "You are right. This is your castle and I have no right to intrude. Nevertheless, I am without a horse and need a place to stay for the night. If you don't want me here, I would be satisfied with sleeping in your garden."

"No," Adam replied, forcing his words to be filtered and polite. "I would . . . enjoy your company . . . if you desire to stay."

"Thank you."

The monster only growled in reply. Belle quickly turned the conversation to the castle. "Dark though the halls may be, this castle seems to resemble the place in which our monarchs used to dwell. We have some older people in our village who were blessed to see the inside of the king and queen's castle, and I am utterly amazed how this place fits the description they so often weave in their tales. When I was younger, I always dreamed of meeting the monarchs, but my father told me that they were killed many years ago, and then their son was soon after killed in battle. Our village has been without a ruler ever since."

"Your monarchs died bravely. Was their passing mourned?"

Belle did her best thinking sitting down, but she did not dare lie on the floor. Trying her hardest to remember everything her father had told her about the past monarchy, Belle replied, "*If* I am remembering correctly, the king and queen were greatly mourned by my father's generation. Why do you ask?"

"Curiosity," Adam mumbled. His excuse was poor, but that was the first reason that he thought to give. "And what of their son, the prince?"

"If you wish me to say that he was given the same respects as his parents, I am afraid I cannot. I unfortunately have very few memories of my past, and I cannot remember my father ever mentioning the former prince in kindness." Belle paused, slowly remembering bits of information that she had heard over the years. "In fact, I think our village despised the prince and did not shed a single tear over his passing."

"You mean your village had little compassion for the prince? Was he not just a young lad when he . . . died?"

Belle shrugged. "I cannot speak for the entire village. I can hardly speak for myself."

Adam cleared his throat, which sounded like a churning bucket filled with gravel. "Thank you for answering my questions. I have been in this place for such a long while, I sometimes miss major events that occur in the outside

123

world." Taking a moment to pace, Adam continued the conversation. "So I assume you have come for the others?"

"Others?"

Adam stopped and began clawing at his own face. The Beast inside of him was raging and screaming. *"She lies, she lies! She has come to free the others so that they may join together and kill you! They know you are the Prince, and they are tired of living under your rule. You are a worthless piece of refuse, and no people would ever want to be ruled by you. Join me and we will kill her together while there is still time! We will rip this wench into shreds, showing the others what will happen to them if they dare rebel. Remember how satisfied we feel when blood is spilled?"*

The prince threw himself against a wall with great force. Adam had learned over the years that, when he really did not care to listen to the Beast, physical pain would silence the monster's voice. This would jar his focus and cause the Beast to retreat for a while, but Adam had yet to figure out a way to silence the Beast for more than a few hours. Many of Adam's scars, cuts, and bruises were all self-inflicted, serving now as little reminders of all the times he tried to banish his inner monster and failed.

Adam kept slamming his body against the wall until he felt he was on the verge of unconsciousness. The Beast was thankfully silenced, albeit for but a moment. Unfortunately, Adam's strange and unexplained frenzy had frightened Belle incredibly, causing her to run deeper into the castle. Now Adam had to track down another unwanted guest. At least he had the advantage; Adam knew the castle inside and out by heart. The girl would not know where to turn.

Chapter Fourteen

Prisoners

Belle was running. She did not know where she was running to, but she was moving as fast as her legs would carry her. Belle was leaving her path of escape almost up to chance, not caring whether she turned right or left, just as long as she ended up somewhere far away. With every jolt her frantic pace would bring, Belle cursed her own stupidity for entering the castle. She recalled each story she had ever heard or read and tried to remember what to do when caught alone inside an enchanted or haunted castle. Unfortunately, the only memory she had told her to *keep running*.

As soon as the creature started throwing himself around the room, Belle had begun to back away. When the monster – *"What had the garden called it? The Beast?"* – yowled and screamed in rage, Belle knew her time had come to leave; but she did not dare to leave through the same door from whence she entered. If she made her exit through the garden, the closed iron gates would certainly trap her. Belle held on to the hope, her only hope, that there would be another way out of the castle.

Belle continued to run and run. Left, right, up the stairs, down the hall, and around every corner she ran! Belle wanted to get as far away as she could. Back on the first floor, the monster's mumblings had been almost impossible to understand, but Belle did pick up a few words that she wished she had not heard; the creature had called her a lying wench, or something similar. Belle had answered truthfully when she conveyed that she did not know anyone else who would dare to come to the castle, but obviously, the creature did not believe her.

Belle began to lose track of how many flights of stairs she had encountered, but by the ache in her legs, she knew she had climbed quite a few. Feeling momentarily safe and extremely tired, Belle slumped against a wall. Her breaths began to come in ragged pants, but they soon slowed down to mild sighs.

"H-hello? Has someone come to help us?"

Belle felt as though her heart jumped up into her throat and then fell down to her stomach. Belle was sure that she recognized the caller, but here, the voice sounded out of place and almost foreign. Slowly getting on her hands and knees, Belle crawled around another corner, only to discover that the room in which she had chosen to rest was the castle's prison!

And, surely enough, Belle's assumptions were correct: the girl who called out was her sister, Lilly!

Belle did not waste a second in running to the cage in which Lilly and Seymour were being held. Pressing her face against the cold iron bars, Belle stretched her whole arm through one of the narrow gaps, trying ever so hard to reach for her sister. Burning tears ran down Belle's face as she drank in the scene. There was her only family, behind bars, caged like filthy animals.

A single shaft of moonlight seeped through a crude window, illuminating the cell in an eerie fashion. Lilly's hair was covered in dirt and her dress was ripped and frayed around the hem and shoulders. Her eyes were wide with fear, and she looked to Belle for help. Belle began to weep when she realized why Lilly did not come over and grasp her outstretched hand: Lilly was kneeling by the farthest wall, cradling their unconscious father. Belle strained her eyes to see how badly he was hurt; blood stained his hair and his forehead was horribly wounded.

"How –" Belle began, but could not choke out more than one word.

"We were ambushed." Lily's voice was cold and wavering, traumatized by the past events. "We had lost our way and thought the castle courtyard would be a good place to set up camp. We were soon taken in as trespassers and imprisoned like thieves."

"Oh, Lilly..."

Lilly turned her head away from Belle and looked at her father, who was beginning to stir. In that brief moment of time, after Lilly had looked away and before their father awakened, Belle was overcome with the most burning flame of hatred she had ever felt. She hated the monster that hurt her family. She hated the castle for being deceivingly inviting, and yet so deadly. She hated whatever map her father must have used for being so ambiguous and confusing. But most of all, Belle hated herself. If she had gone with her family, she could have perhaps prevented all this from happening. If she had agreed to marry Caspar, she would have the hope that her fiancé would come and rescue them all. Now Belle felt like she had no hope, only hatred; still she prayed for a miracle.

"Lilly?" Seymour was finally waking up.

"I'm here, Papa. I've been here all the time."

"Is Belle here?"

Thrusting her body forward, Belle tried to reach deeper into the cell. "I'm right here, Papa, right here. I won't leave."

"Would you go put Philippe in the barn, Belle? He's been in the pasture all day."

And all was silent for a few moments. Everyone, though they were separated by iron, was glad to be with their loved ones. Though neither spoke a word, both Belle and Lilly could tell what the other was thinking: they needed to get their father to Monsieur Cartier, or else they would be orphans by sunrise. Belle, making sure her voice was as low as a whisper, asked Lilly if she had any matches in her pocket. Lilly agreed that she did, but they were damp and broken. Belle asked for them anyway.

Belle knew that the monster would find them eventually and she wanted to be prepared. After finding a few broken slats of wood, she tore the hem of her dress and wrapped the cloths around the tips of the sticks; Belle then proceeded to blot the matches with her shawl until they were decently dried. Then she waited until she heard the thundering footsteps of the Beast coming towards them. She was finally able to light her makeshift torches after a few failed attempts. When the monster rushed into the prison room, Belle was standing by the cell, brandishing the torches.

"You think I am going to be scared off by a little fire?" Adam began to walk closely to the girl. He had to admit that she was brave to try to stand up to *him*. "*One swipe, right across her throat. Remember how powerful you feel when blood is shed.*" Adam did not even try to block out the Beast's tempting words. Minding to stay enveloped in the shadows as much as possible, Adam crept closer Belle.

"Do you think I will be scared off by your threats?" In all honesty, Belle was terrified. If this *thing* was mostly animal, then he would be able to smell her fear; Belle did not want to give the creature any sort of advantage. Mustering up as much courage as was humanly possible, Belle said, "These two are my father and sister. Release them!" With great force, Belle jabbed her fiery stick into the shadows, hoping to burn any part of the hated creature's flesh. She missed and tripped over a raised brick on the floor.

As she fell, the torches flew out of Belle's hand and sailed across the room. By the time the sticks landed on the floor, their lights had gone out; the room was now completely dark and silent, except for the glinting glow of the monster's eyes and the vehement exhalations of his breath.

"New deal," Adam cried as he unlocked and threw open the door to the cell. Lilly screamed as the monster rushed towards Seymour, grabbing the man by the collar of his shirt and dragging him out into the center of the room. Lilly tried to claw at the thing that was taking her father, but was soon forcefully kicked into a corner. Belle screamed in rage after hearing the crunch of bones as Lilly landed on the floor. The Beast was unperturbed by all the shouts and screams!

"Alright, old man. Now your time has come to make a choice. I will let you and *one* of your daughters go free. You can decide which one goes home with you and which one stays here." Pulling the man's head back by his hair, Adam laughed, "You're fortunate enough to have two daughters; you wouldn't mind sharing one with me?"

Seymour, who was still delusional from his earlier concussion, replied very foolishly. "Oh, Belle's not really my daughter."

Chapter Fifteen

People in the Castle

Two months had passed and Belle was still in the castle. She had grown accustomed to the abysmal dreariness of the palace and to the gruffness of her *master*. But, as she curled up on her bed, Belle realized that she had not recovered from the shock of the past events.

"*Oh, Belle's not really my daughter.*"

Belle started to cry, again. After the third week, she stopped counting the times that she let her tears flow. "*Why did they never tell me? Why did they think they were right to lie to me all these years?*" She curled into an upright ball and rocked away her tears. Belle had been living out these last few months moving in and out of depression, bewilderment, loneliness, and the overwhelming feeling of unwant. However, one thought plagued her above the rest: "*I have no purpose. If I am not a Dubois, than who am I? I am no one.*"

A lonely tower bell began to chime. Sighing, Belle pushed herself off her bed, which still had an unwanted amount of dust underneath the surface. This was her one-thousandth, four-hundredth, and seventieth hour of serving the Beast; one of her "bedroom's" walls was covered in little white scratch marks where she kept track of every hour that she was forced into servitude.

Fetching her little apron off an old coat rack, Belle ran downstairs to the main hall where the monster was waiting for her. She slowed down as she neared the room where the Beast sat. Lowering her head and staring miserably down at the floor, Belle said good morning for the sixty-second time. The room was always same. A fire roaring in the fireplace, one so ferocious that Belle did not dare to enter.

Every day, she only stayed in the doorway and did not take more than a few steps into the room. There were always shadows dancing and playing about the room, flirting with the fire's light. The only thing in the room was a high-back chair that was placed right in front of the fireplace. In that chair sat the Beast, his back towards the door and his eyes toward the fire.

"Fetch me water," demanded the Beast. "And you should probably start waking up earlier."

"I will."

Adam growled in disgust. "I have asked you to call me 'master.' I thought you would have learned that by now."

Belle bit her tongue until she tasted the metallic saltiness of blood; a little drop pooled in her mouth. She never thought that she could ever hate anyone, but over the past few months, Belle had taught herself to loathe and despise the Beast. She had never seen actually seen the creature's face, but she had heard just about enough of his voice. If Death, Hatred, Vile Thoughts, and Disgust could all be given a voice, their voices combined would sound like the Beast.

He always spoke coldly, which made Belle sometimes pity him; she knew no one could be born with such an ugly heart, so Belle believed that something must have happened to him in the past, something so terribly awful to make him into the vile creature that he was now.

"Well? Are you going to just stay in here all day?"

"No, master." And Belle turned to leave.

So far, Belle had been drawing water from the well out in the garden. That day, however, was a bitter autumn day, so Belle decided to see if there was an indoor pump; she knew that the richer people in the village had indoor pumps installed in their kitchens, so Belle knew that was the first place she should check.

By a process of trial and error, Belle finally found the right door that led to the kitchen. The room was dark, but there was enough light seeping through the windows for Belle to slightly see. But after walking through the door, Belle discovered something more frightful than the lack of an indoor pump: she discovered people!

Belle screamed in shock, for she had assumed that, after two months of solitude, she was the only servant in the castle. But there were at least twenty persons in this room alone! After the surprise wore off, Belle's heart melted in relief, ecstatic that she would not have to spend her days by herself. She approached the closest woman to her and began to introduce herself. The woman was bent over, her plump backside facing Belle, and she seemed to be fiddling with something in the oven.

"*Bonjour.* I'm . . . well, I guess you could say I'm new here, even though I have been living upstairs for well over five weeks. Pardon me for asking, but how was I not aware of your presence? I thought I was the only servant here. Oh, but now I do not have to be alone; you have no idea how lonely I felt, thinking I was the only one in this entire castle, besides the Beast. Mind if I ask what you are baking?" Belle paused for a considerate amount of time, but the woman did not respond in any way. "Madame? Did you hear me?" Finally, Belle decided to move on to another person in the kitchen.

She first tried to speak to the girl who was reading a cookbook while beating something in a bowl; but (Belle assumed because she was concentrated on reading the recipe correctly) the girl did not converse with her. Belle ran around the room trying one person after another, but no one would talk back to her. Driven to tears, Belle screamed at the group as a whole, begging someone to talk to her.

"*Are they ignoring me because I am not a hired hand, but a slave? Are they judging me because I am no more than a prisoner instead of a maid?*" Desperate to receive just a little attention and hopefully make a friend, Belle continued to make her way around the kitchen, talking to everyone whether they would talk to her or not.

"Mademoiselle, have you lost your mind?"

Belle whipped around, frightened to see the monster's looming figure filling up the doorway. He stepped closer to her and she began to cower, knowing how violent he could become when provoked to anger. Belle looked down at the floor and pushed her hair behind her ear; she had been told once that when a girl pushes her hair behind her ear, she is either conveying a flirtatious or innocent spirit. Belle was hoping to go for innocence, for she thought that an innocent act and smile would appease the creature's rage. She had no such luck.

"Speak to me when I ask you a question!"

"I was just trying to talk to the other servants, ma–"

The Beast laughed, which was more comparable to a cruel bark. "You are crazy, to think that they would *talk* to you."

"I'm sorry, but I thought that, if I presented myself as another servant instead of a slave, they would befriend me."

"Do you think you have the magic to make the dead speak?"

Bewilderment covering her face, Belle looked up from the floor. "I . . . I don't understand."

"Of course you don't," Adam muttered. After turning halfway out the door, the creature called back, "There is a candle on the far table and a box of matches beside the window. Light the candle only after I am gone. The light should help explain the situation."

"Why can't I light the match while you are in the room?"

"The light will hurt my eyes," Adam lied. While this was partly true, Adam could have easily adjusted to the dim light of a candle. What he really did not want was for the girl to see him. Adam was disgusted with himself and his appearance, and he was sure that the slave, if she saw him too, would be equally as disturbed and frightened. He left the kitchen, his secret safe for another day.

Belle waited for the door to close before she ran to find the matches and candle. After lighting the candle and waiting for the flame to grow brighter, Belle looked around the room. Belle had never believed in ghosts, witches, or anything of the like, but standing in that kitchen, Belle believed that places could truly be haunted and people could really be cursed.

Despite being bathed in the flickering glow of the candle's flame, the room felt dead. Belle quickly understood why none of the people had responded to her conversations: they were all statues, each carved in the same intricate detail as the statue in the garden. All throughout the room there seemed to be elements of movement; the flowing hem of a skirt, the frothy waves of beaten eggs, the turned heads of servants calling out to one another, and yet, all was still.

Every person in the room was no more than a carving of stone, and everything that they held or touched was part of the statues as well. Belle was astounded by how real everything appeared to be. *"It's as if,"* Belle thought to herself, *"everything was alive and then suddenly everyone was turned to stone, right in the middle of their movements."* That thought made Belle's stomach sour.

For the rest of the day, Belle went about her chores, feeling as though every statue in the palace and on the grounds was watching her. Later that night, while sleeping on her dusty cot, Belle writhed in the natural, but was completely still in her dream. She stood again in the kitchen as she watched the statues come to life in a frightful fashion; their limbs twisted eerily, their necks bent at abnormal angles, and their jaws hung slack. Their stony hands reached out for Belle as they slowly advanced toward her, their feet scraping across the floor.

"What do you want with me?" Belle screamed.

"We were once living," cried one of the figures.

"But now we are stone," finished another.

"What does that have to do with me?" Belle inquired of the statues.

Together, all the statues chanted, "You have a choice. Fear us, and everyone shall remain as they are, or you could visit the West Wing. Your findings will set it in motion."

"Set *what* in motion?"

As the statues returned to their previous positions, their limbs and necks twisting back into place, they breathed out, "The lift of the curse."

Belle awoke with a start, gasping for air and yearning for peace. All was silent, but Belle could still here the voices in her head, begging her to go to the West Wing. "I will," Belle whispered. "But not tonight." She thought that the castle was eerie enough in the daytime; she did not dare discover how haunted the place could become when the sun went down. But she firmly said, "When tomorrow comes, I *will* visit the West Wing."

Chapter Sixteen

Guilt and Miscommunications

Caspar had never felt so miserable in his life, except for maybe the time he had been tracking down a rare, fifteen-point buck and then lost the blasted creature to a hungry grizzly bear. However, both instances had shown Caspar that he did not enjoy being denied the good things in life, especially when he had spent so much time trying to obtain them. Three years he had spent with Belle only to find out that she did not love him! And she had told him so callously. Did she not care that his heart would break?

"Here's another round for you, Caspar."

Caspar mumbled a drunken, "Thank you," and proceeded to drain the ale. *"The benefit of owning a tavern,"* Caspar thought to himself as he stared into the murky, amber liquid pooled at the bottom of his glass, *"the drinks are always free!"* Turning around on his barstool, Caspar leaned back on the counter and surveyed the room.

He had always seen himself as a better man than the slobs and slovenly rift-raft that walked through his door. That was, after all, one of the reasons why he had opened the tavern: to give a fine meal and a hearty stout to the weary traveler and to be an example of a true man to those who found themselves falling into the less-than-perfect category of life.

But now, after two months of living with and brooding over a broken heart, Caspar was beginning to see these men in a revolutionary light! They had all come to bury their griefs, sorrows, and aching hearts in the worldly cure of liquor. Caspar laughed as he pictured his mother and father trying to tell him that the church, in the presence of Christian brethren and God, was the only place where one could find peace. Sneering, he remembered that Belle held similar beliefs. In an act of defiance, Caspar took another long swig of his beer before leaving the counter to go mingle with guests and customers.

"Uncle!" Caspar cried as he made his final round through the tavern. "How long have you been here?"

Cartier frowned and his voice was burdened with grief. "I have been here long enough to see you stumble about the place like a drunken fool." Reaching out for his nephew's shoulder, Cartier whispered, "Let's go home, Caspar."

"No," Caspar shouted as he pulled back from his uncle's grasp. "*This* . . . this is my sanctuary! Dare you take me away in my time of mourning?"

"Sit down, Caspar."

"I don't care to do so at this moment."

Cartier Chantelle was a man of few words, but when he did speak, those who listened heard a voice that spoke with power and authority. Cartier was a gentle man, but gentle does not mean weak; there were times when Cartier had shown a strength more powerful than a young man half his age. Placing his hand once again on his nephew's shoulder, this time with a vice-like grip, Cartier replied, "Sit. Down."

Caspar heeded the command, the look on his face similar to that of a petulant child. But Cartier did not come to scold Caspar, he only came so he could talk to his nephew and perhaps give him a piece of sage advice. "Two months have passed, Caspar."

"I know."

"How long will time go on before you see Belle again?"

Caspar looked away from his uncle in attempt to conceal the tears in his eyes. "She seems to be just fine with the separation." He breathed out a shaky breath before continuing. "She has not even come to the village since I –"

"Lost your temper and frightened the poor girl?"

"I was going to say 'proposed.'"

Cartier took a moment to find a chair. Sitting down, Cartier leaned forward and looked Caspar directly in the eyes. "Caspar, Seymour seldom talks with me anymore. Belle has not been to my bookstore in ages. The Chantelles and Dubois have been friends for quite a few generations; I'd hate to see all that go to waste and ruin because you won't amend your friendship with Belle."

"She broke my heart."

"She was being honest with you, Caspar, just as you should be honest with yourself right now. Ask yourself this question: do you want to continue to brood, building up your resentment and hatred, or would you rather try and fix what has been broken?"

Caspar paused for a moment, truly contemplating his answer. "She doesn't appear to be too keen on fixing things either," he grumbled.

Resting his head in his hands, Cartier rubbed his eyes wearily. He was trying to teach forgiveness and gentlemanly manners to a stony heart. Cartier let out a deep and troubled sigh before asking his final question. "Who called for the separation?"

"Well, I did, but –"

"Then that's your problem! Belle probably hasn't spoken to you yet because she thinks that, since you initiated the time apart, you'll have first say on when the separation ends. Out of her respect for you, she is keeping quiet so you can have your time to brood and think."

Raising his head and smiling for the first time in weeks, Caspar looked at his uncle. A passionate hope began to burn in the young man's eyes. "You . . . you really think that's the reason she hasn't come to the tavern?"

"I do indeed. Now, I would suggest going over to the Dubois house right this very instant. Don't let another day end without the two of you reconciling."

Caspar jumped from his chair, his muscular frame nearly knocking down a table. Shaking his uncle's hand enthusiastically, Caspar cried, "I will, Uncle Cartier. I will go *right* this moment! Thank you ever so much. You helped to clear the fog of depression from my head and heart." With a fervent bolt for the door, Caspar started running to Belle's house.

On his way there, Caspar berated himself for not seeing the situation clearly until today. *"How could I have been so dense? She has kept quite out of her respect for me! After all, who in their right mind would not respect and adore a man such as myself?"*

Lilly sat in her bedroom, which had become rather dreary quite suddenly. She was surprised to find how lonely a room could feel when one of the beds was empty all the time;

Lilly continued to freshen the bed each morning, hoping there would be a head on the pillow by nightfall. At dawn, she would rise, pull the sheets off the Belle's bed, shake them out, and then continue to make the bed in proper fashion. One morning, Lilly did something special as she fluffed the pillow: she kissed the white linen cover as she whispered, "I love you."

Sitting back down on her own bed, Lilly gazed out her window and tried not to cry. She shut her eyes as she remembered the day Belle came into the Dubois home; Lilly prayed that if she remembered and relived that day as much as she could, she could bring Belle back home. But alas, as she opened her eyes, Lilly came to realize that simply remembering Belle would not bring her back.

Tears pooled in Lilly's eyes and sobs choked her throat as she remembered the same thought that had been plaguing her mind for the past week. Every day a little voice inside Lilly's head would remind her of how dire things were, saying, *"How awful that I gained a sister and best friend in one day and lost both in one night."*

Of course, Lilly was not the only one grieving. When they had left the castle and for their first few days at home, Seymour had not known the complete details of Belle's absence. But finally, after his head trauma had cleared, Lilly forced herself to tell her papa the truth about Belle's situation. Lilly, up until the night she sat Seymour down and told him why Belle was not at home, had never see a grown man cry. She had never seen anything more rendering before in her entire life.

As she tried to console her father, Lilly came to one conclusive thought: *"Women, young or old, can cry about many things. And whether their tears be shed for things trivial or important, to see a woman or girl cry is much more normal. I now think that men cry only when their heart is truly crushed. And when you see and man cry for the first time, you can't help that your heart breaks a little too."* And so Lilly wrapped her arms around her father's heaving shoulders and remained there until dawn.

A bright red silhouette brought Lilly back to the present. Slowly moving away from her bed, Lilly tiptoed to her window and discreetly pulled back her curtain's edge. She happily sighed when she realized that the stranger's form belonged to Caspar. He was pacing back and forth in front of the door, his face scrunched up in indecision, like he was unsure of whether or not to actually make his presence known.

Lilly was relieved to see a friendly face; after their incident in the castle, Lilly began to see little bits of hideous monsters in every face. But as she secretly gazed upon Caspar's face, Lilly knew that she would never find a more handsome man. Sitting back down on her bed, Lilly hummed as she waited for Caspar to knock on the door; she planned to wait a few seconds before answering the door (she didn't want to appear too eager). But as the reverberating knock echoed throughout the small house, Lilly was sickened as she remembered whom Caspar had come to see: his sweet Belle! Lilly took no time in running to the door.

"Lilly, please. Don't."

The girl's feet stopped almost instantly, but her body continued to slide forward for a moment. Lilly turned to see her papa's bulky form slumping in the worn-out living room chair; Seymour hadn't moved much from that spot for the past few days (after he had learned about the part he had played in sending Belle to her doom, Seymour fell into an incurable, mind-numbing depression). Placing her small hand on his arm, Lilly tried to explain to her father that she would be a rude host to keep a man like Caspar waiting on the doorstep.

But, despite his current situation, Seymour still could see through his daughter's words. "Don't tell him about Belle," the old man pleaded.

Tears filled Lilly's eyes. "I cannot lie to him, Papa! Caspar would form a rescue party if he had the slightest notion that Belle was in danger; he might be Belle's only hope."

Seymour looked at Lilly with eyes like a mournful dog. "I am a horrible father."

"Papa, that wasn't your fault! Your head was injured; you could not make decisions for yourself!"

Despite his daughter's pleadings, Seymour did not seem hear a word Lilly said, he just stared at the wall as if that was the only thing he could see in the entire world. "Caspar is the closest thing I have to a son."

"And wouldn't you want your son to be brave and rescue any maiden who was in danger?"

"I would be sending him to his death if I asked him to travel to that accursed castle."

"But he would rescue Belle!"

With that, Seymour leaped up from his chair, grasped Lilly's tiny frame, and shook her. "Don't you see? Belle is dead!" Then, as if he had not considered the weighty meaning of his words until after he finished speaking, Seymour fell to the ground, silently crying. Lilly knelt down beside her father, whispering in his ear that everything was going to be fine. As she helped him back into his chair, Lilly promised that she would not tell Caspar the truth about Belle's disappearance. But she did go and talk to the man anyways.

Taking a deep breath before she opened the door, Lilly glanced heavenwards and apologized for the lie that she was about to tell. Then she had a brilliant idea! Lilly would tell Caspar the most ridiculous lie, one so absurd that the man would immediately know she was fabricating a tale. Then, after he would press her hard for the truth, Lilly would be able to tell her father that she had been forced to explain to Caspar the real account of Belle's absence. So she opened the door, her incredulous lie already planned out. "Hello Caspar."

"Oh, Lilly. You look lovely today. Um, is Belle here?"

Lilly cast a glance over her shoulder and decided that she should close the door so that her father would not hear their conversation. "No, Caspar, she isn't. Belle decided that she wanted to live with a handsome, young man at a castle far away. She is quite happy where she is, much happier than she was here. I do not think she would ever come back. I cannot believe that she waited until now to leave; you should really see the castle! The rooms are so spacious and the gardens are just lovely." Lilly plastered a sappy and sweet smile across her face, hoping that Caspar would see through the facade.

Unfortunately, Caspar had not ever really acquainted himself Lilly, so he took her words to be truth. He broke his eye contact with the girl to glance at the door, hoping that Seymour would come to clarify. But the old man never came, so Caspar simply nodded and said he understood.

Here was where a grave miscommunication took place. Lilly, when Caspar said he understood, thought that the man had seen through the lie and already discerned the truth! This was great news to her; she had gotten her point across to Caspar without breaking her promise to her father. She clasped his hands with her own and gleefully cried, "Thank you! Oh thank you, Caspar, for understanding. Belle will be so very pleased. You have done us such a great favor. Now you must rally a great army; Belle's captor is just one monster, but still he is strong. I am forever in your debt. Thank you for going to rescue my sister!"

But Caspar had already shut his hears to Lilly's words. He had slipped immediately into a rejected and deaf-like state of mind when he learned Belle was gone. And his stomach soured at the thought of his girl living with another man. In a castle, no less! He did not recognize his feelings right away, but the unbearable seed of jealousy was starting to take root in his heart. He mumbled a farewell to Lilly and headed back to the tavern.

Chapter Seventeen
Enemies Still Living

Cartier had been sitting outside the tavern, waiting for his nephew to return with joyous news of Belle's and his reconciliation. He smiled at the passing people, trying to ignore the judgmental glances they gave as they passed the tavern; the pub was already known as an indecent and rambunctious place, and Cartier knew he was not doing his own reputation any good by sitting right by the front door. He knew he would have to seriously talk to his nephew about turning the tavern into a more respectable avenue of business.

As Caspar neared the door, Cartier could immediately see that things did not go as planned; his nephew was utterly crest-fallen and his shoulders slumped miserably. Cartier could not think of a single word that would console Caspar, so he instead just placed a loving, understanding hand on his nephew's shoulder.

Cartier hated the tavern ("An ungodly den of miscreants," he had once said), but the man knew Caspar was in no state to be left unattended in a place where beer was just as abundant as water. He stayed by his nephew's side all night, even sitting beside him at the bar. After hours of unbearable silence, Cartier finally spoke. "You might feel better if you talked –"

The sound of a wooden mug crashing on the floor caught the attention of every man in the tavern. "Talk? I am tired of talking, Uncle! I have tried talking to her." Taking a breath and quieting his voice, Caspar continued, "She was not even there to greet me."

"Then why did you not search for her? Surely she is somewhere in the village!"

"She was not! She has left the village and decided to live some well-to-do man up in a faraway castle." And when he had thought no one could hear him, Caspar mumbled to himself, "Her perfect fairy tale dream come true."

Louis Alexandre, who was known for his lack of common sense and at the time was filled with well over two pints of ale, chuckled to a friend, "Never thought Belle would be the kind of girl that would give her away her virginity with such ease. Not that I would mind being the lover who found his way to her heart." That was the man's first grave mistake.

Caspar was on top of his cousin in a second. Grabbing the man by the edges of his jacket, Caspar lifted the low-life out of his chair and threw him across the room, completely forgetting that there was any familial relation between them. Everyone leapt to their feet, ready to join into the brawl at a moment's notice. Louis crashed into a few tables, but soon found the strength to get up and turn to face Caspar (his second mistake).

"If I hear you speaking of any woman, especially Belle, in such a vulgar way again," Caspar growled, his eyes burning with an ardent rage.

"So what? You know that it is true! She has probably secretly been a whore this entire time, and who would blame her? She has the kind of figure that deserves to be shared, if you know what I mean." Louis laughed at his own joke. Unfortunately, he did not know when to shut up, and this most recent statement was the man's third and final mistake for the night.

Moving at an alarming speed, Caspar launched himself at Louis and swung a dangerous right hook. The disgusting crack of a broken nose echoed throughout the room. The cad fell back to the ground and earned the wisdom to stay down. Caspar lumbered above him, casually wiping blood off his knuckles. "Say one more word," warned Caspar, "And I will see you personally thrown out of town. I care no longer that we are cousins; you have made yourself a fool this very night." Louis nodded and, clutching the remains of his nose, ran out of the tavern; he would spend the rest of his days trying to win back Caspar's respect.

Some of the words Louis said lingered with Caspar. Now doubt was working inwards towards Caspar's heart, fatally mixing with jealousy. The tavern returned to normal soon enough. All the patrons returned to their tables and quietly huddled together, fearing that anything they might say or do could enrage Caspar even more. But there were two men sitting at a table in a darkened corner who had witnessed the entire fight but did not react in any way. They had just sat in their chairs, with the hoods of their cloaks pulled high over their heads, and listened; what they heard had pleased them. The scrawnier of the two looked at his companion and motioned towards the door.

"I think we s-s-s-should vis-s-s-sit this-s-s-s cas-s-s-stle, don't you?"

Four Years Prior

Enno gasped for breath as he pushed himself up from under the heaped pile of bodies. His pointy nose curled into a disgusted sneer as his senses realized how *dead* his own body smelled. Of course, hiding under a plethora of rotting corpses will alter anyone's natural body aroma into a revolting stench. Enno continued to climb out of the pile, all the while his eyes searching for human soldiers that might be rounding a nearby corner. He hoped that he was not the last of his people alive, but as he saw how many of his comrades lay strewn in the streets, Enno came to terms that he might be last fairy on the earth.

"Enno? Is-s-s-s that you?"

"Anno! How bles-s-s-sed I am to hear a familiar voice that is-s-s-s not crying out in pain. Where did you hide all this-s-s-s time?"

Anno waddled over to Enno. "Inside of a fis-s-s-sh barrel. Though the experience was-s-s-s horrendous-s-s-s, I mus-s-s-st s-s-s-say I think I fared better than you. I am very glad to s-s-s-see that we are both alive. Perhaps-s-s-s we s-s-s-should take this-s-s-s unfortunate event as-s-s-s an opportunity to expand our riches-s-s-s-s?" The two brothers clasped hands and proceeded to scurry about the town, taking any goods that their neighbors were obviously not going to use any longer.

Once they had filled their arms with stolen treasure, the two fairies doubled back around to the royal palace just in time to see two men and a boy come out through the immaculate wooden doors. Anno's chubby hand immediately went for the dagger that hung at his side, but Enno stopped him. Pointing to one of the men, Enno exclaimed, "Look what the human creature holds-s-s-s in his-s-s-s arms-s-s-s!" They were both disgusted and mortified; there, in the arms of one their enemies no less, lay the wings of their beloved employer and honored queen.

Creeping closer, Enno and Anno also realized that the queen's body was not with the men. Now the two fairies could be terribly dumb at times, but when they saw the young boy light a torch and point towards the castle, they both new where they were to look for their queen. And because they had been Jezé's personal assassins, they knew of a secret entrance in the back of the castle. They quietly bypassed the guards, hearing a little bit of a heated argument as they rounded the side of the building and found the secret door that was hidden under a tangled mess of ivy.

They made their way to the main room of the palace and saw the dark, crumpled form of the queen lying in the middle of the floor. Enno and Anno rushed to Jezé; they cradled her head and held her hand, well aware of how frigid and pale her skin had become.

"My . . . servants."

The two fairies cried out in fright and alarm, but soon begged for forgiveness; though she was dying, Enno and Anno still feared the queen, her explosive wrath, and her despise for fear. They knelt as close to her as they dared. "My queen," Enno politely asked, "who did this-s-s-s to you?"

"Tell us-s-s-s, my queen. We s-s-s-shall avenge your blood!" Anno thrust his dagger into the air to make his point even more clear.

"The boy. He did this to me! Never let . . . him rest. He will most likely . . . go back to his castle after he . . . finishes his conquest here. Find him in a . . . few years and end his miserable life!" Jezé coughed, ruby red blood covering her lips as she did so.

"Why s-s-s-should we not go out there and finis-s-s-sh the boy now? Give the humans-s-s-s a reas-s-s-son to fear us-s-s-s again!"

But the fairies were the ones who were filled with fear. Suddenly the cavernous room erupted with flames and smoke. The queen coughed again before talking for the final time to her servants. "Let the boy . . . believe he is safe for a few years. He will most likely . . . suspect an attempt at revenge. Wait, and he will be . . . completely surprised by his own death. Now go! Leave me here –"

"Death by fire is-s-s-s not fitting for a queen like yours-s-s-self!"

"I . . . I am already dead. A cremation is . . . not so horrible."

The beams above were being to crack and buckle. Neither of the fairies felt right about leaving the queen's body, but if they tried to carry her out, no one would survive the inferno. As the flames rose higher, the two decided that their window of escape was closing drastically. Kissing their queen's hand for the final time, Enno and Anno fled for the secret door.

Enno told himself not to look back, but he did; after exiting the door, Enno turned around to see his queen be engulfed completely in the flames. He did not see everything correctly at that moment, but in later years, when thinking back on the accursed night, Enno would swear that he possibly saw another figure struggling though the flames, trying to reach Jezé.

"S-s-s-so what do we do now?" Anno asked once he and Enno were at a safe distance away from the fairy village. Once the building had started collapsing from the heat of the fire, he started running into the forest as fast as his chubby legs would take him. Anno was never a lover of exercise and self-exertion (unless there was blood to be spilled), but he was smart enough to know when to run for his life. Now, hidden away in the bushes, he was bent over and gasping for precious breath.

Enno, who was not panting nearly as hard, replied, "We wait. Just like the queen s-s-s-said. We will know when the time is-s-s-s right to exact our revenge."

"But . . . but what do we do until that time? Our homes-s-s-s are des-s-s-stroyed; we have nowhere to go and live!" Anno continued to blubber on about how he refused to live as the olden fairies once did, making homes in the trees and in underground holes. He required a suitable shelter!

"There is-s-s-s a human village not too far from here; we could s-s-s-settle down there –"

"If you haven't noticed, brother, we are fairies-s-s-s. We won't exactly blend in with thes-s-s-se humans-s-s-s."

"Your dullnes-s-s-s of mind frightens-s-s-s me s-s-s-sometimes, Anno. Have you forgotten all that our queen taught us-s-s-s? Don't you remember that we have the power to take on any form? I s-s-s-say we go to this-s-s-s village, trans-s-s-sform ours-s-s-selves into human-like beings-s-s-s, and live there until the time comes-s-s-s."

Anno agreed to the plan. "And who knows-s-s-s, Enno? We might even find someone to help us-s-s-s in tracking down and killing this-s-s-s prince!"

Chapter Eighteen
The Bloody Discovery

Belle, though trepidation haunted her throughout the day, willed within her heart that she would keep her promise and visit the West Wing. Knowing that the monster had made a habit of visiting the garden every night at dusk, she hoped that he would stay out there for a considerable amount of time, for she wanted at least half an hour to explore the West Wing. So, she waited. As was expected, Belle heard the large castle door close shut as the sky turned from rosy pinks and lemony yellows into foreboding, musky blues and purples. Her adventure was free to commence!

Knowing she did not have much time, Belle only brought one candle along with her. Belle hesitated before leaving her little corner of the castle; she knew where the West Wing was, but she had never felt the freedom to explore there. Her master did not even like to talk about that part of the castle, and he had even gone as far as to forbid her to visit the West Wing. However, none of his threats mattered to Belle anymore; she was going to the West Wing and she was going there now!

Belle had never explored any part of the castle at night, and as she crept along the stairs and corridors, she now knew why; somehow, after the sun had gone away, the castle seemed to take on a scarier persona. The statues looked a little more hideous. The many stairs appeared to be deadlier than before. Every little piece of furniture looked as though another disfigured monster could be hiding behind them. Taking a deep breath to calm herself, Belle decided that she would not be afraid and that now would be a perfect time to light her candle.

The tiny flame of light helped immensely! Belle sighed in relief as she realized that light, no matter how small, helped the castle look as normal as before. "*Well,*" Belle thought to herself, "*As normal as a cursed castle can look.*" Belle continued to walk on with purpose, determined to reach the West Wing before the Beast returned.

Now, more than ever, Belle missed her family; she had always thought that when she finally received her chance of adventure, her father and sister would be there beside her. She thought of how she would feel now if Caspar was the one to complete this mission with her. For a slight instant, Belle almost began to cry, remembering what their friendship had once been like.

"I wonder if he misses me as I occasionally miss him. He has probably become the village favorite, still wearing the guise of a charming gentleman. I wonder how the people would treat him if they knew of his arrogance and temper. Still, I'd rather have him by my side than explore this castle alone." As she walked the darkened hallways, Belle realized that there were some quests in life she had to conquer by herself. Holding the end of the candlestick a little bit tighter, Belle lifted her skirts and ran to the West Wing.

Even though this part of the castle was entirely knew to Belle, she seemed to know exactly where to go, as if some predestined instinct suddenly bloomed in her heart. She knew to choose the left stairwell instead of the right. When she reached the end of the hallway, Belle had no internal dispute over which door she must enter. Her instincts and courage had led her thus far, but as she reached to open the door, her bravery faltered.

"This is silly." Belle scolded herself. *"I am a grown woman of seventeen years, and yet I'm afraid to open a simple door!"* Scoffing away all her worries, Belle pushed open the door.

The room to which the door led was probably the dirtiest, most torn-up part of the castle. Chairs lay splintered on the floor, while shredded curtains and tapestries hung from the walls. Belle had to carefully navigate her footsteps, for shattered vases and pottery were another part of the room's ornamentation. Finding her way proved to be a harder task than expected because the candle's flame was quickly dying.

The light did indeed go out, but Belle was not left in the dark for long. On a table in the center of the room there was a source of silvery light, beautiful enough to wane any fears, but magical enough to arouse hesitations. As Belle approached, she discovered that the light was coming from a shard of glass about the size of a palm. The light was indeed silver, comparable to gorgeous shafts of moonlight; there were also slivers of an emerald-like glow that mixed with the light. Belle stared at the glass for such a long while that she thought saw the faint image of a dying rose reflected in the center of the shard; however, she told herself she really couldn't see a rose in the piece of glass.

The light from the shard was faint, but it allowed Belle to see adequately. The first thing her eyes happened upon were some words carved into the table's center: SBLA RSE. Belle studied the letters form for a minute or two, tracing her fingers over the indentions. The letters themselves appeared to have been chiseled into the table with a knife or other sharp tool, and the writer must have been very hasty in his work; Belle could make out the beginning of other letters, but not enough to have comprehension of the words. Deciding she had lingered long enough, Belle picked up the piece of glass and continued around the room.

"*NO! He truly is a monster.*"

For years to come, Belle would wish she had just left the room when her candle's flame snuffed out. Perhaps if she had only stayed at the table, or remained in her room, she would have never been forced to witness the most horrendous sight.

Wings, myriads of wings, hung by crude nails all over the walls and littered the room. Helmets, breastplates, bows, and swords were piled on tables and benches. Tears flowed down Belle's cheeks, which were flushed in anger and fear. She knew immediately to whom the wings belonged, and judging by the fading stains of blood, these wings were taken by force. Knees weak, Belle collapsed to the floor and stared in disbelief at the sight she beheld. As she soaked in everything, one thought penetrated her amidst all the confusion and rage: "*He's real. The Fairy Gobbler is real.*"

Belle knew that fairies were gentle, peaceful creatures, which, for the most part, wished no harm on any person. True, there were a few villains mixed in with the good, but the majority of fairies were passive forest-dwellers. With this information in her heart and mind, Belle knew that the fairies did not lose their wings in a battle they had initiated; no, she realized that the fault fell upon the very monster that dwelt in the castle. Even as she heard the thumping footsteps of the Beast drawing ever nearer, Belle's fear gave way to a boiling anger.

"What are you doing here?" The monster roared as he all but charged through the doorway. "I should rip you in pieces right now, and I will, if you don't return to your room this instant!"

Unfazed by his violent threats, Belle stood her ground. "You would dare to murder so many innocent fairies? Have you no heart? I thought I had learned to hate you, but what I felt then was only mere dislike compared to what I feel now. *This* is my hate!" To emphasize her anger, Belle took a step closer towards the monster and flung the shard of glass towards what she hoped was his chest. Apparently, the shard was more precious to the creature than Belle had thought, for after he had moved aside to avoid being struck, the monster lunged quickly to catch his possession.

The light instantly vanished as the Beast wrapped his massive hands around the piece of glass. He turned toward Belle, only letting her see his gleaming eyes. Adam no longer cared about trying to treat the girl nicely, a decision that made the Beast grow stronger. Drawing himself up to his full height, Adam and the Beast, yelling as one, bellowed, "Leave! And never come back."

In her heart, Belle screamed in return, "With pleasure!" No audible words, however, left her mouth. Eyes widening in fear, Belle finally realized that she would be foolish if she tried to stay at that castle any longer. She quickly retreated from the West Wing, thankful for the opportunity to leave. Running towards the garden, the maiden thought to herself, "*I hope he dies alone and miserable.*"

Mental anguish attacked Belle as she left the castle. She all too painfully remembered that Philippe was no longer with her; thankfully, Belle knew of a single mare that lived in the stables. She was surprised that the poor horse had not been mauled or torn to pieces as of yet, but knew the horse would sooner or later be made into a meal for the monster. Belle realized that the mare had the same inclination, for she readily helped Belle in escaping the castle grounds.

Belle quickly became extremely fond of Antoinette (the name she had seen carved over the mare's stable). She was not as old as Philippe, but the majestic way she galloped through the woods was astounding for a horse her age. Antoinette rode with purpose, and she knew to whatever destination she rode would be better than the castle.

You may be wondering why Antoinette is still a live horse and not one made of cold, breathless stone. The answer is simple: she was not at the castle when Enchantress spoke the curse. Antoinette was spared only because she was in the right place (the forest) at the most opportune time.

I suppose now would also be a sufficient time to explain *why* Enchantress turned the entire castle's servitude into statues. She did so because she could not predict Adam's beastly behavior; she did not know if the monster inside of the boy would hurt or even kill the persons in his castle. She needed everyone to still be in the castle, but not live in fear for his or her life. Reminders of Adam's past needed to be constantly before him, yet Enchantress did not want the servants to be forced to witness the prince's gruesome transformation.

Therefore, turning everyone into statues was the safest and most logical choice. Everyone in the castle, as Enchantress breathed out her last few words, was immediately frozen in time. When and if

Adam repents and banishes the Beast from his heart, then stone shall be replaced by flesh, and each and every servant will take a breath as though they exhaled only a second ago. Not one moment will have passed for them.

But enough talk of stone statues and what might become of them. Let us return to Belle and her escape.

Belle had never run away from anything before. As she felt the heavy thump of her heart and the hard jolt of Antoinette's galloping stride, Belle decided that she hated running away. Belle knew that she would have probably died if she had stayed and faced her attacker, but she hated how the act of escaping ignited the fire of her fears.

The daunting forest into which she rode did not settle her anxieties in any way. The early-autumn snow that had fallen was too icy and pale to be considered lovely or serene. And because the snow was such a frosty white, the trees, in comparison, seemed almost pitch black; their long, bare branches reached out for Belle like hungry monsters hunting in the night. Most frightening of all were the occasional pairs of eyes Belle would see leering at her from behind a tree or from inside a bush.

Finally, Antoinette slowed her pace. The mare had been locked away for so long, surviving only on the weeds and rainwater that would collect in the stable, that she was almost too weak to run for an extended period. As soon as she felt the cold snow beneath her hooves, however, and after she had been given her chance of freedom, Antoinette forced herself to gallop as long and fast as she could bear. Unlike Belle, the horse had no qualms with running away; Antoinette did not want to spend a single moment more in her shabby excuse of a stable.

Belle had not exerted herself as the fair horse had just done, but still her heart pounded and her breath came in strenuous gasps and pants. "Thank you, Antoinette. You have done extremely well. Perhaps we should –"

Belle did not even have the opportunity to finish her sentence. Eyes, eyes of creatures who once appeared to be far within the shadows, slowly began to move closer. One howl rang out to Belle's left, resounding like a frightening call-to-arms. She had occasionally heard a wolf's howl when she was younger, but at that time, Belle had been in the safety of her own home. Now, with the wolf no more than twenty feet behind her, she realized how deadly a predator's howl could actually be. She knew there was no possible way she could ever outrun a pack of wolves, but Antoinette thought differently.

Snow wildly flew into the air as the mare galloped through the forest, mad with fear and deranged with empty hope. Belle realized the smart thing to do would be to jump to the ground and quickly climb high into a tree; she could not, however, bring herself to abandon Antoinette. The poor horse had given so much of herself, and still she pushed her legs harder to carry Belle to safety. *"No,"* Belle reckoned within her heart, *"whatever the outcome be, I shall endure the same fate as Antoinette."*

Belle was sure that her time had come. The wolves had easily caught up with their prey, and they began to snap greedily at Antoinette's heels, enjoying every fear-filled cry that left the horse's mouth. Most of the wolves were only interested in the mare, but two seemed strangely fascinated with Belle. One leapt up and, entangling its teeth in her shawl, pulled her to the ground. The largest wolf howled; soon the entire pack was completely focused on Belle, each one wanting to go in for the kill.

But Belle was not one to surrender easily. When she was yanked off Antoinette, Belle landed beside a large, broken tree limb. Gathering all courage and strength, Belle poised herself for battle; she swung, crushing the jaw of the first wolf that sprang towards her. She knew that she could not fight off every one of the wolves, for such a hope was unrealistic. Belle expected death at any second.

The wolves eventually overwhelmed Belle, pinning her down against the snowy forest floor. She began to cry as she thought of all the kisses she would never be able to plant on her father's cheeks, of all of Lillie's stories she never would hear.

Belle was disgusted with the two largest wolves, which were obviously the leaders of the pack; they paced slowly in front of her, drawing out the moment to an unnecessarily long length of time. They toyed with her, snapping just inches away from her face. Belle thought her ears were playing tricks, for at one point, she thought she heard the wolves laugh. She thought she saw them smile when she had screamed in fear.

"*Please, God. Send me help.*" Belle offered up her prayer shortly before she closed her eyes and gave up struggling. Cold, sharp claws quickly wrapped around her chest and throat and her body was thrown deeper into the snow.

Chapter Nineteen

An Unexpected Rescue

"*Foolish girl!*"

Adam screamed long and loud, infuriated that the girl had disobeyed his orders. He had told her never to set foot in the West Wing, and there she was! He should have killed her or at least bitten off an appendage. "*Foolish girl!*"

Yet amidst his rantings, Adam knew, in whatever tiny portion that was left of his heart, that he had been the foolish one. He should have never told the girl to leave; she was not Sabella Rose, but Adam had secretly hoped she could play a part in his monster's undoing. However, the Beast had so polluted Adam's mind, cunningly helping the lad to believe he was in the right. "*You don't need the girl. You do not have to respect her. She is your prisoner; treat her as such!*"

The Beast was content in letting the girl leave. He had often felt threatened in her presence. Adam, on the other hand, had already begun to miss the girl, Belle. Running to the shard, Adam whispered, "I wish to see the girl." His heart broke as he realized that the girl was not only a far distance from the castle, but she had escaped with Antoinette also.

"I told you we should have killed the horse! If we did, the girl would not have been able to get so far away. We would have been able to track her down and kill her."

Adam, depressed and ashamed, turned to leave the West Wing. But before he could walk through the doorway, something made him turn back to look at the piece of glass; a curious, somber feeling came over Adam as he realized that this glance would be one of the last times he could look at the girl. True, he could summon the mirror to show her face at any time, but because the Beast gained new strength every day, Adam doubted he would even remember her by sunrise; the anger in his heart would erase all memories of her goodness.

Adam looked back at his magical mirror, and to his amazement, the picture changed ever so slightly. Belle and Antoinette had stopped, right in the middle of the forest! *"Why does she stop? Does she not fear that I could easily track her down?"* He smiled as he saw a panicked, terrified look come over the girl; perhaps she did fear him after all.

The Beast, pleased that he had been successful in embedding fear in the girl, attempted to leave; Adam, however, wanted to watch. Then he heard the sound. Wolves howled as they caught sight of the horse and girl. Adam wasted not a single second in chasing after Belle. He had lost his parents to wolves; he was not going to let those savages claim another life. He knew his chances of reaching Belle were next to none, but still he had to try.

Like the pulling of reigns on a charging steed, the Beast tried to make Adam stay in the castle. He tried yelling, ordering, and even cursing. The Beast even attempted to tell Adam to stay, knowing that the young man's mind was temporarily geared to do the opposite of what the monster commanded. Adam ignored every word, and told himself that he would save Belle, and no sadistic, inner creature could make him do otherwise.

Adam ran to the forest, all four of his limbs thumping the ground in a wild, rhythmic pattern. Twice, he heard the wolves howl again. The hair on his back rose at the noise, for the howling sounded too familiar. Flashbacks to that awful night pounded in the prince's mind, bringing tears to his eyes once more. Adam told himself that past was not important, and that he needed to keep his mind focused on rescuing Belle. He knew he was close when his nose burned with the stench of wolf musk. When he eventually saw the pack, he himself felt like howling in victory, but thought he should keep the element of surprise on his side.

And surprise the pack he did! Adam, claws out and hair bristled, leapt from the bushes with speed and fury. Even if the wolves had been prepared for an attack, they could not have fended him off. Adam's first instinct was to go for the wolves themselves, to kill as many as he could as quickly as possible. But when he saw Belle lying in the snow, fearful to the point of unconsciousness, Adam knew she first had to be protected. Trying to be wary of his claws, Adam attempted to gently lift the girl. Finding a little snow mound, Adam placed Belle safely away from the horde.

"*I'm coming for you, wretched thieves,*" Adam thought as he turned towards the wolves.

Adam fought hard, clawing one face and bighting another. One time the wolves did overcome him, but Adam did not let them win; in groups of two and three, he sent the pack scurrying. Finally, only two remained. They were the biggest wolves, but Adam was not frightened. Letting out a roar, one neither bears nor lions could match, Adam charged the remainders.

The fight was short, but definitely fatal. The fatter wolf lost a paw, while the other one's eye was brutally met with the monster's claws. Adam did not go without injury; both wolves were able to get in a considerable amount of bites and scratches before being lifted in the air and flung deeper into the forest. Neither one returned. Feeling faint, Adam limply fell to the ground. The last thing he saw was the young woman, running to Antoinette.

Belle woke at the very end of the brawl. She was completely disoriented, and as the shock of the cold snow against her back began to fade away, Belle first thought was to set her feet to flight. She quickly found Antoinette, her reigns tangled in a bare bush. *"I must leave this haunted place!"* But something tugged at her heart to turn around. She did not know why, but she felt peace in delaying her escape. Laying one hand on the neck of the horse, Belle turned around slowly.

There she saw him. The monster, her enslaver, lay on the ground with his face in the snow. The sun had been asleep for hours, and there was very little moonlight, so all Belle could really see was a mass of hair and blood. *"Blood."* There was too much for Belle's liking, but she appreciated the wounds the Beast took for her. Telling herself that he would be fine, Belle smiled and turned to leave.

"But to where do I go?"

During her time at the castle, Belle had deeply begun to miss her family and friends, but as she prepared the horse for the journey, Belle asked herself if they were ready for her. Perhaps Seymour was ready for Belle to come home, but ever since the denouncement, Belle constantly wondered if she could ever go back to the Dubois; she felt like she was deceiving herself in thinking that she could go back home and everything would be fine. *"Could I go back to living in a lie?"*

Then there was Caspar, but Belle could not fathom how awful a life with him would be. Belle resigned to believe that he might make a decent, protective husband in a few years, but not for her. Considering how long she had been gone and how they parted under such unfavorable terms, Belle would not be surprised if she returned to the village to see that Caspar had picked another gal to be his wife.

"After all," Belle smiled as a thought entered her head, *"All the girls already fawn over him. He would only have to 'Would you,' and every young woman in the village would cry 'Yes!'"* And with her mind on Caspar, Belle thought of kind Monsieur Cartier. The older man would willingly open up his home to her, but Belle knew that Madam Louise would be rather upset.

Belle thought next of Lilly. For as much of her life that she could remember, Lilly was the nicest person that Belle ever knew; and, until a few months ago, Belle would have had no hesitations in rushing home to her sister. But now she paused because her heart was having a difficult time in justifying Lilly's actions. *"How did she manage to lie to me?*

And how long has she been telling me I was her sister, even though I wasn't?"

Belle remembered the one incident that she never felt had been clearly answered: the time in the forest when she was supposedly playing, hit her head, then had to be retaught all her childhood memories. Belle was not convinced for certain, but she began to believe that day was the day she became an adopted Dubois girl.

After she had run through a list of everyone she knew, Belle could not think of a single person or family with whom she could comfortably live. She finally made up her mind that she would ride until she found a village unknown to her and then start a brand new life, but something held her back. Turning around, she realized that it was not something that held her heart, but *someone.*

As she looked again at the monster, Belle was overwhelmed with compassion. Though she had not seen the battle, she was moved to tears at the thought of the creature fighting for her life and safety. Despite for the hateful feelings she still had for the Beast, Belle could not bring herself to leave him alone in the freezing snow.

So, Belle brought Antoinette over, close to her master. She, after much pleading and convincing, managed to get the mare to lay down in the snow so that Belle could push the

Beast onto Antoinette's back. Thankfully, the woman was not as physically weak as some might have thought; though the task took a few moments to complete, the maiden was able to get the creature on top of Antoinette's back. "Back to the castle, girl. Your master has some wounds that require some attention."

Though Antoinette was hesitant to walk into the castle, Belle told the horse that she would give the horse some lumps of sugar if she agreed to help the creature. The horse only went as far as the drawing room, allowed Belle to remove the burden from her back, and then trotted back to the courtyard. Belle quickly started working, mending the monster's wounds; she felt silly for trying to be nice to the Beast, but she told herself that every creature should be shown some amount of kindness.

She ripped some strips from her dress, which was unfortunately shortening in length to the point of embarrassment. Finding a pot and two lumps of sugar in the kitchen, Belle ran to the garden. Giving Antoinette her well-earned sugar, Belle filled the pot with snow; she then went back inside, started a small fire, and began to boil the snow-water.

Bringing the pot and rags into the drawing room, Belle was surprised to find that the creature was up and already beginning to lick his wounds. Not wanting to startle him, Belle rapped gently on the doorframe and coughed politely. "May I help you with that?"

Adam was not startled, but he was surprised. When he woke up, he had assumed he had dragged himself back after the fight, and then fainted on the couch. To hear that Belle was still in the castle, *and* she was willing to help him with his wounds, was a complete and utter shock. "Why do you want to help me?"

"Those wounds will fester if they aren't properly cleaned. A doctor friend of mine taught me how to clean wounds, and, if you will let me, I'd like to do so."

With a ruff grunt for reply, Adam let Belle come over and take care of his injuries, but first hid all but his wounded arm with a heavy blanket. The boiling water burned, and Adam let Belle know of his discomfort. His muffled voice screamed out from underneath the blanket, "Could you please clean these wounds in a less painful way? I have already been through enough discomfort, having to go into the forest to rescue you –"

"Well, I had not intended to be attacked by wolves!" Casting her eyes downwards, Belle timidly continued, "Master, I have served you well so far, may I ask one thing of you?"

Adam was hesitant in responding. The Beast told him to snap off the girl's head and put an end to her annoying and pitiful peasant life. Then something else, perhaps the last bit of good in Adam's heart (or whatever little bit was left of his conscience) told him he should treat this girl with a little more kindness and respect. "Belle, was your name, correct?"

Belle nodded. She did not like how the creature said, "*Was* your name," but she had no right to argue with him. Since Seymour's renouncement of her, Belle had many times wondered what her name really was. So, instead of correcting the monster's choice of verb tense, Belle stayed quiet and stared into the shadows.

"Anyway, Belle . . . I have noticed that, yes . . . you have served me well. I could not have asked for . . . a better companion." Adam was disappointed in himself that he could no longer speak kind words without a struggle. Ugly words, hateful words, they all came easily, but nice phrases and sincere compliments were extremely hard to say. Still, Adam pressed on and finished saying what he knew he had to say. "In reward for your hard work, I . . . will grant you one request." But after realizing what he had committed himself to, the Beast quickly interjected, "Except to leave! I will allow you to do anything but leave this castle."

"I . . . wasn't going to ask permission to leave. I have nowhere to go to if I was to leave. I do not care for this castle, but I have no other home. What I was going to ask is this: may you show yourself to me? For two months now, all I have seen is your shadow. I felt your hand and face when I first arrived, but I ask now if you will show me yourself. I doubt that you understand how degraded I feel when I have to address a shadow as 'master.'"

All was quiet for what felt like eternity, but then Belle heard a low rumble, and quickly stepped away as the creature's cover flew off. Belle was able to see the crest of a head peeking out; after he stood, Belle could still only see the monster's shadow on the floor. But for the first time, Belle noticed how much the shadow resembled the shadow of a man. The creature stood still, but the shadow seemed to dance, moved by the flickering fire.

"I do not think the decision to show myself to you is a wise one," Adam explained, and for the first time in an extremely long while, both Adam and Belle heard timidity in Adam's voice.

"I promise not to show my fear, and I will not run away. I don't even have a home to where I can run."

"*Go ahead,*" the Beast dared. "*Show us to the miserable wretch of a girl! Frighten her just as we have frightened others.*"

Against his better judgment, Adam started to move his feet. His steps began small, but the creature soon began to gain stride. Adam stiffened his back and squared his shoulders. He told himself that, if he could not walk with pride in the state of being he was in, he had no right to be proud as a human. "Nothing can prepare you for what you will see," Adam warned the girl.

Belle inhaled deeply and braced herself, trying to stiffen her legs; she willed herself not to faint, no matter what she would see! The fire started to dim, causing Belle to strain her eyes to see the monster. "*Perhaps the lack of light is a benefit,*" Belle thought to herself, "*I won't see as many details.*" She did not know how wrong she was, for Adam had become a creature of the night, and his most frightening features seemed to become more illuminated in the dark.

The first things that Belle saw were two massive feet and abnormally large hands. The creature's toenails had turned yellow and green on the tip, and they were long and jagged; his fingernails were not extremely discolored, but they were covered in bits and pieces of gore from his late night prey.

As the monster slowly walked out of the shadows, Belle saw his arms. The young woman had to put a hand to her mouth in attempt to choke down the bile that was slowly rising in her throat. Belle had never seen anything so disgusting! Hair, wiry and ungroomed, covered the creature's arms, shoulders, and neck; no one could count how many insects had infested the overgrown mass of hair.

And then she saw his face, and for possibly the first time in her life, Belle felt an overwhelming sense of fear, mingled with compassion. She could tell that the creature originally had beautifully smooth skin, but she could not draw her eyes away from the scars and bruises that fought for their place on the monster's face. The two massive fangs forcing their ways out of his mouth contorted his face structure. Belle saved looking into the creature's eyes for last. They, the eyes' irises, were a frightening mixture of brown, gold, and red; the pupils were as black as coal and glassy as a polished onyx.

But Belle saw layers and such a depth of emotion in those eyes that she had never seen in any others. As she looked, she first saw hatred and disgust. Searching deeper, she saw the complexities of mistrust, confusion, and denial, accompanied by loss, fear, and a longing for love. Here Belle realized something of extreme importance: both the creature and she felt misplaced in this life. Neither of them had a family, but yet they knew they needed love. They were both seen as outcasts by society, yet they were both still searching for a place where they could belong.

"Thank you," Belle whispered.

"For what?" Adam asked.

"For showing me your face. I now know what you look like, and I can now better understand your behavior."

"You're not frightened? Disgusted?" Adam was shocked that this girl was still standing, still speaking to him. How could she look at him and not show her contempt?

"I might have been," Belle said. But taking a moment to look intently at his eyes, Belle continued, "But now I see there is more to you than the monster I see before me."

Adam held Belle's gaze. The warmth in her eyes, the kindness that she was willing to show, and the bravery she was modeling comforted him. For years, Adam had felt like his heart had been decaying, eaten up by his anger and depression. But this girl's gentle spirit began to revive his heart; Adam felt for the first time that he could learn to love again!

Chapter Twenty
Old, Familiar Faces

Both wolves stood on the forest border. They were afraid to turn into their original selves, fearful of how their freshly inflicted wounds would appear. The wolves cowered among the trees; neither knew where they should go, only where they could not. The one wolf that lost his paw finally accepted the loss, bent over, and begun to lick his wound. When he could no longer bare the metallic and salty taste, the wolf spat and growled in disgust. "Well that went wonderfully well," Anno barked, not caring to tone down the contempt in his voice.

The other wolf, Enno, glared at his comrade, though not as well as he would have liked. His right eye had been all but gouged out of his face, and a nasty cut split his eyelid. But still, Enno stared with his most intimidating look. "Things-s-s-s would have gone better if you had not been s-s-s-so eager in attacking the girl! S-s-s-she is-s-s-s nothing is the grand s-s-s-scheme –"

"You and your s-s-s-schemes-s-s! You forget that my current form becomes-s-s-s hungrier quicker than my true s-s-s-self."

The two bickered until the early hours of the morning. Even as dawn approached, their accusations towards one another did not wear down. They probably would have stayed there, arguing in the forest until the end of time, if not for one idea that wormed its way into Anno's devilish mind. "Our mis-s-s-sion," he began, "Is-s-s-s to kill the Prince, but this-s-s-s Beas-s-s-st of the forres-s-s-st is-s-s-s in our way."

"He wouldn't be, if you had not gone after the girl! He obvious-s-s-sly cares-s-s-s for the maiden."

"Nevertheles-s-s-s, we cannot even reach the cas-s-s-stle unles-s-s-s the mons-s-s-ster is-s-s-s killed. Why not go to the village and recruit men to kill the Beas-s-s-st?" Anno smiled, proud that he himself had devised such a clever plot.

"That is-s-s-s a fair plan, but the human men will not follow us-s-s-s into battle – which is-s-s-s what we will have if we got to fight this-s-s-s creature." Enno began to pace as he considered other possibilities. "What if we pers-s-s-suaded one man to help us? He would be our front, the face behind this-s-s-s war!"

Anno considered the question and quickly responded. "Who would we choos-s-s-se?"

"What about the tavern owner? I have obs-s-s-served him, and I know he has-s-s-s much anger in his-s-s-s heart. If we can convince him that he s-s-s-should channel his-s-s-s hatred towards-s-s-s the Beas-s-s-st, we would have a winning ally!"

"But how will we convince him that the mons-s-s-ster is-s-s-s his-s-s-s enemy?"

Enno was surprised that he did not have an answer to Anno's question; but since he did not want to damage his pride or his position of being the wiser fairy, Enno simply decided to answer in a very cryptic fashion. Rubbing his chin, he whispered, "Oh I have s-s-s-something deliciously evil planned. Though the details-s-s-s are not completely clear, I promis-s-s-se that man Cas-s-s-spar will do our biding willingly. We will follow him; I am quite s-s-s-sure that s-s-s-something in his-s-s-s life will lead way to him hating the Beas-s-s-t with extremely."

"Would you like to have a tour of the castle?"

This was the first question Adam had asked politely for the past seven years; he had always recognized the needs for manners when his parents were around, but after they had died, Adam never asked for anything. Commands, demands, and accusations were the only sentences he knew how to speak. But now, though he had not yet realized why, Adam was beginning to change for the better. True to his word, he never went back into the shadows. But still the prince did not know how to treat Belle any nicer than he would the servants of his castle. He was learning, though the process was painfully slow.

Belle was noticing the change as well, but she also saw where more improvement was needed. She, however, never lashed out at the creature or tried to fix his faults herself; she believed that change was something one had to do on their own. But she did praise him for when he showed kindness or humility, and a day did not go by that she did not thank the creature for saving her from the wolves.

"Yes, I would. All except for the West Wing, though. I wish never to see that part of the castle again."

"If you so wish. Come, there are things you need to see."

Adam first led Belle to the North Wing. Belle thought that the North Wing was in the best condition. "The floors are fairly clean, the curtains are whole, and the furniture isn't destroyed. This looks like an entirely different place," she mused.

"That is because I . . . do not come here often." Adam was embarrassed by his own voice; sadness and depression hung on every word he spoke as he talked about the North Wing. This had been his parents' favorite part of the entire castle. Tradition was that every king and queen of France would dance their first dance in the wing's ballroom, and Adam recalled how mesmerized he had been when his father described his dance with Princess Marie.

Adam had once looked forward to the night when he could whisk a young maiden out onto the floor and dance his way into a happily-ever-after romance; he now knew that was a hopelessly lost dream, because he was hideously disfigured, and the ballroom was forever occupied.

"What's in here?" Belle, perhaps quite by accident, was actually pointing towards the room's ornate doors.

"That's the ballroom." Adam bit his tongue, hoping that Belle would not want to explore the room, though he knew she would. No girl would ever pass up a chance to view a royal castle ballroom, though the room was far from regal or glorious. And before he could say otherwise, Belle pulled open the door and ran inside, unaware of the horrors that awaited her.

The chamber was filled with people, as a ballroom should be, but not a single one moved. These were the remainders of the servants, all of whom had been turned into stone. As Adam had spent the night ravishing the fairy village, the servants had gathered in the ballroom for a small celebration of Mr. Worthington's retirement, and they were still there. Smiles were frozen on faces; glasses, held high for toasts that would never be completed, were suspended in the air.

Adam was disgusted how a room full of dead people could look so cheery. The somber, macabre feeling that hung in the air made his soul restless. He had first been upset that the servants had used the room without his permission, but now he would give next to everything to fill the room with laughter once more.

The prince found Belle standing in the center of the ballroom, running from statue to statue, gazing at their faces and aweing over the complex details. Adam envied her ignorance; she was not scared with the knowledge of what these statues really were. He walked slowly, hating the questions he knew he would soon have to answer.

Belle greeted him with a smile. "This . . . this is a strange way to occupy a ballroom. Why do you have so many statues?"

Still not trusting Belle enough, Adam dared not tell the girl the truth. "They used to keep me company." Pausing for a moment, Adam continued with, "They all have names. And there is a story to tell of each one."

Belle sighed, excited as if she was living in a fairy tale, completely forgetting the horrors of the West Wing. Grasping one of the creature's hands, Belle asked, "Would you tell me their stories?"

Adam consented and began to show Belle every statue. He was surprised to find that he actually remembered every one's name and the pleasant memories attached to them. There was the little farmer who, on happy occasions, would bring one hundred freshly picked apples to the castle; he always said he came to bring tribute to the monarchs, but Adam knew the rumors of his romance with one of the maids.

Then he showed Belle the footmen, the horses' trainer and grooms, the florist, and every other person worth mentioning. Adam mainly was the one to lead, but Belle would sometimes personally pick out a statue that intrigued her. Coming upon a slender statue with a beaming smile spread across his face, Belle stated, "What a handsome man! Come, tell me, what is his name?"

"That is Jean Claude Pierre. And you are in the right to call him handsome; no girl can resist his charm. He is my jack-of-all-trades; he keeps me company, works in the kitchen, takes excellent care of each and every guest, and is a marvelous entertainer."

"Why look! If you gaze into them long enough, you can see the twinkle in his eyes." Belle was enraptured by how alive these statues could appear.

Looking around, Adam saw the reason for the joviality in Jean's eyes. "Follow his gaze," Adam said as he positioned Belle with her back towards the statue, "And look straight through that small crowd of people."

Belle did and saw a young woman who was bent over a table, feather duster in hand. "Who is that?"

"That would be Estelle, sauciest maid in the castle. There are many times when she could verbally cut any man down, just because he gives her the wrong sort of look. But Jean Claude she loves; she is his fiancée."

"Then this man has good reason to smile. Whose story shall we hear next?"

Adam led Belle to a statue, one whose face was older, but nonetheless happier. "This is Mrs. Agatha Kettlery, best nurse to ever raise me. She is loving, caring, and sweet; she could cheer up just about anybody with a single cup of tea and the occasional lump of sugar. She is the maids' manger, so to speak, though she never flaunts her position.

"Her parents are of British descent, and though she loved her home very much, she was sent to work here in France at the age of fourteen. She would have stayed a barmaid if not for a kind queen that offered her a job as a nanny. Agatha Comberstone then came to the castle to care for a young princess, my mother, and later married the handyman, Mr. Joseph Kettlery. She spent every day repaying the kindness my grandmother showed her."

"She looks motherly," Belle sighed.

Adam laughed before saying, "She should! Has had over fifty children in her lifetime here at the castle."

"Isn't that a bit impossible?"

"Well, they weren't all *her* children. My parents, since they were monarchs, were often called upon for help by provinces that had experienced war or famine; many young ones were sent here to the castle, not only to be put to work, but also to be given a home. Mrs. Kettlery took each one under her wing and raised them as her own. She did, however, have a few children herself. Five, to be exact. The youngest one is out in the garden."

"Timothy! I . . . met him when I first arrived." Tears came to Belle's eyes as she recalled the day. "Poor child looked like he had many sorrows in his heart." After a long moment of silence, Belle enquired, "Can you show me one more? I am beginning to grow tired, and would very much like to go to bed."

"Certainly." Quickly searching the room, Adam found one more statue that would be the perfect one on which to end the night. "Here he is! This is one man you must meet!"

"He looks . . . almost humorous."

The statue did indeed make Belle and Adam laugh. The poor fellow's portly stomach bulged from under his waste coat and an oversized pocket watch dangled from his pocket. A thin mustache, one as thin as copper wire, hung above his upper lip and twirled outward, framing his rotund cheeks. Yet, despite his jolly appearance, the man looked absolutely uptight; Belle did point out that there was a little bit of happiness in his eyes. "*Almost priggish,*" Belle thought to herself, and yet she still smiled. No matter how much of a stickler this man was, she could not help but love him. "And who is this man?"

"That is Mr. Worthington, overseer of all the castle's functions. He is a perfectionist, and is absolutely miserable when things are not in precise order. He has been employed here at the castle since my father's father was a young man. Mr. Worthington is actually the reason why everyone is gathered here. He was planning to retire, though I feel we would have all convinced him to stay. He had a fascination with clocks and machinery of the like. Everybody joked about he should be a clock himself, and he would simply reply, 'That would be impossible.' Poor man never understood the necessity of laughter."

Belle sighed again, struggling to concentrate. She was feeling wilted and tired and decided that she had to go lie down. But before she left, Belle drew up the courage to ask one more name. "You have been excellent in recalling all the names of these statues, but there is one more name you have forgotten to tell."

"And what name would that be?"

"Yours. Please, tell me your name. I shall still call you 'master' if you like, but I would very much enjoy knowing your name."

"Adam. My name is Adam."

Chapter Twenty-One
Telling the Truth

"I can't do this any longer!"

Lilly loved her father dearly, but he had nearly drained every ounce of patience within her. For close to half a year, Seymour would only stay deep inside the house or his workshop. Lilly hated to see her papa's mind deteriorate, but she was sure that guilt was rotting him from the inside out.

Lilly was also disgusted how not one person in the village had even batted an eye at or inquired about Belle's disappearance. Before the entire ordeal took place, Lilly had heard whisperings of how many of the women wanted Belle to leave town anyway; poor souls were probably thinking their wish had been answered, not bothering to think there may have been a more dangerous explanation.

Sitting down beside her father, Lilly calmly stated, "Papa, you can't stay locked inside the house forever." Lilly sighed before continuing. Today would have been Belle's eighteenth birthday, and as her present, Lilly swore to start setting things aright. "We lied to Belle about her origins; we were wrong to let her believe she was always a Dubois. But we are committing an even greater injustice now! Please,

Papa, please. Tell Caspar of Belle's captor. Prove to me that you love *both* of your daughters."

Seymour's eyes slowly began to sparkle; the captive fog that glazed his pupils and clouded his mind was burned away under hope's cleansing fire. "I will," he cried. "Yes, yes! And they will help me, too! Caspar will know what to do. He will fell that Beast! Oh that hideous creature will rue the day he took us captive." Grabbing his hat and cloak, Seymour ran to the tavern. As his feet carried him away, Lilly heard him shout, "Kill the creature! The Beast has got Belle."

Lilly stayed standing in the light of her own home. She was finally glad to see her father do the right thing. Lilly sighed, relaxing for the moment; for the first time in nearly a year, she believed her heart coming together as a whole. As she felt time repair her heart piece by piece, Lilly promised that nothing would ever break her again.

But one horrible thought did break through her peace. Recalling the look in her father's eyes before he rushed out the door, Lilly remembered seeing more than just a look of hope. There had been something else, a lurking wildness, which had hidden itself within Seymour's eyes as he ran around cursing the monster.

"They'll think him mad!"

"*What a life,*" Caspar thought to himself. He had a tavern to call his own, a doting aunt who gave him free room-and-board (the occasional lecture had become tolerable), and a myriad of villagers who gawked at his very presence. True, he was still upset about Belle's disappearance, but not as disappointed as he pretended to be.

Caspar feigned his heartbreak, and his friends did all in their power to cheer him up in return; they gave him gifts, called him a hero, and even praised his very name. Caspar would occasionally show a lift in his spirits, sometimes by saving a damsel from a runaway carriage or a child from a dangerous bear, and the people would become increasingly endeared to him.

But there was still an unresolved amount of jealousy in his heart. He always told the people that Belle would be his wife, but inside, he knew that would never be true. Some days he secretly swore that if he ever met the man who stole Belle's heart, he would slaughter him by any means necessary. Anytime Caspar thought of Belle's new lover, he would turn absolutely bitter, almost to the point of intolerance, but this just made the people appease him more.

And so, Caspar sat in his tavern, thinking how lucky he was to have so many friends. He laughed as Louis pranced about the tavern, running flasks of beer back and forth to

Caspar. *"The poor fool,"* mocked Caspar. He had never been all too mad at his cousin, but because Louis thought he had to work to repair his relationship with him, Caspar now had a personal servant; life could not be sweeter.

"Caspar!"

Everyone in the tavern quieted down as the old man stumbled into the tavern. His skin was pale from the cold, but his cheeks were flushed and his eyes were vibrant. He ran around, grasping each man by the shoulders, shaking them until they understood that he needed help. "Beast," he kept shouting. "Monster!"

"Seymour," Caspar grabbed the man. "What's the matter with you? You look as though you've gone crazy."

Tears pooled in the poor fellow's eyes as he told everyone the truth. "I lied. I lied to you all. Belle did not leave; she was taken! Taken by a horrible creature; so frightening he was, with tremendous claws, perilous fangs, and rage in his eyes that burned like the fires of hell. I am to blame! I let Belle be taken, but now I ask for every able man's help. He is a mighty fighter, but I know a group of fifty men could take him. Please, I can't bare my daughter's absence another day!"

But instead of a rallying cry, the tavern filled with heinous laughter. They mocked and jeered, knowing this *Beast* was a creature of Seymour's own polluted imagination. "He's been down in that workshop of his for far too long," the crowed howled. Everyone was now sure that the old man had lost his mind, and no one cared enough about Belle to consider the possibility of Seymour's words being true.

"Please," Seymour fell at Caspar's feet. "Please tell me you believe me Caspar? If you truly loved Belle, you would risk everything to save her. Please tell these men I am right."

Caspar remained silent for a long time, emptied of any words to say. Something inside of him did believe the man's account, but he feared what the people would think of him if he gave in to Seymour's request. He would be the laughingstock, deemed just as crazy as the old man himself. *"Do I really love Belle enough to risk my standing in this community? And what if she isn't in danger? I trust Lilly's tale more than Seymour's; how foolish would I look if I, along with a small mob, showed up to rescue Belle without cause? She'd count me a fool."*

Turning his back to Seymour, Caspar shouted, "You're crazy, old man, to think that anyone would believe a tale like that one. And just in case you hadn't heard, Belle rejected *me*;

I am not obligated to save her anymore." Nodding to a group of men, Caspar signaled for Seymour to be removed from the tavern.

Deep in the recesses of the room, Enno and Anno stood listening. They, as payment from their queen, had learned to change their forms many times over; now they stood in the corners, appearing to be nothing but a thin cloud of smoke to an observing eye. Both saw opportunity for mischief, and so they struck, moving through the tavern like a trailing vapor.

They whispered lies into the ears of many men, until all were convinced of Seymour's insanity. They knew that his had nothing to do with their grand plan, but the fairies had been working so hard, they could not help but take a break and have a little fun. Tormenting innocent souls had always made Enno and Anno so happy.

Anno came close to Louis. *"You know,"* the fairy whispered for only Louis to hear, *"That crazy old lunatic really does deserve to be put away. If you suggest this to Caspar, he will praise you once again."*

"This story of a monster is preposterous," Enno crooned into Caspar's ears. *"The man's a lunatic! Everyone knows this to be true."*

Louis laughed aloud as he watched Seymour pitifully sulk away. "I see now that Belle's quirks are completely hera . . . here –"

"Hereditary?" Caspar offered.

"Yeah, that. I mean, look at her father. The whole family is probably crazier than we think!"

"*Mph*. You, Louis, are unbelievably correct. I had always seen Seymour as a wise man, much in the likeness to our uncle, but now I think that I was only blinded by my love for Belle."

"Then what say you, men," Louis turned to the crowd in the tavern, "Is Seymour a lunatic?"

A loud, thunderous roar of approval shook the tavern walls. Men threw fists and mugs into the air, as they cried out, "Crazy old man," and "He should be locked away!"

"Put away?" Caspar turned the crowd, shocked by the words he heard. Deep in his heart, he knew Seymour to be of a sound mind, but as the lies were pumped deeper into his brain, Caspar himself actually began to believe that Seymour should be administered.

"I could perhaps help with this," came a voice from the back of the crowd. A tall, lanky man strode forward. He smiled, but not in a pleasant sort of way; his skin was stretched tightly against his bones, and when he smiled, his lips spread and cracked in a tiny, thin line. His complexion was pale, and some considered his pallor to be almost gray. Whatever was left of his hair was white, tangled, and oily. There was a certain stench about him that could cause the bravest of men to turn away. But because he brought forth a solution, he held everyone's eyes and ears.

"What do you suggest?" Caspar never recalled seeing the man before, but if he could somehow prevent Seymour from harming himself or inflicting the village with his senselessness, then Caspar did not really care who the man was.

"I actually own a large – well let's call it a *home* – a few miles out of the village. I take care of the poor, restless souls whose minds are not what they once were. For a price, I could take in Monsieur Dubois. There, he could harm no one with his mindless rantings."

"You propose a valid plan, Monsieur, but I do feel as though we should wait until Belle returns. I would not feel right sending Seymour away without the consent of both his daughters."

"Very well," the man replied, bowing low at the waist. "But remember my offer; I guarantee you will be calling me again very soon."

The man left the tavern slowly, his boots dragging lightly on the floor. He remained solemn, only nodding farewell to a few of the men. But as he reached the outdoors, the man fell to the ground in a fit of evil laughter. Enno rolled and rolled, crying from laughing so terribly hard. Anno soon joined him, and they laughed together. They were so pleased with themselves; they had all but condemned an innocent man to death, and they were reveling in satisfaction.

As they walked back to their abode in the forest, Anno giddily cried, "This is the most fun I have had in years. How wonderful I feel to be wicked again!"

Chapter Twenty-Two
Gifts for Belle

As change came to the seasons, change also befell the castle. The Beast's power was waning quickly, unknowingly abated by each act of Belle's kindness.

Every day Belle grew increasingly beautiful in both appearance and mannerisms. Her soft, brown eyes shown golden in the love she showed to others.

She carried herself regally, but never lost her humbleness. For every spiteful word that was given to her, she spoke only affirmations and compassions.

She had matured into a true beauty.

But there was something in Belle's heart that was deeply hidden, even from herself: bitterness. Though she did find herself smiling wistfully when Adam talked to her, or dreaming how handsome he might be if he were human, Belle still loathed him down within her heart. She had not worked through the hurt and pain she had felt when she had seen the bloody displays of his war.

Whether she does or does not find her way to forgiveness, I cannot say; that would be spoiling a perfectly good story for you to read on your own!

Before I let you return to the story, I hope you haven't forgotten that Belle was – well, she still is, but we are focusing on events that happened long ago – Sabella Rose, fated to wilt like a rose on her nineteenth birthday. The poor dear was experiencing many more withdrawals and fainting spells, and neither she nor Adam knew they had the power to set things right. And unfortunately, neither of them knew that time was of great importance; there was potentially only one more year left of Belle's life.

Now, back to the tale.

Flowers were extremely hard to find in the cold of autumn when snow covered the ground, but Adam had discovered that Belle was well worth the hunt. He spent most of the morning hours searching for what few flowers were left in his garden. Adam smiled as memories of his mother rushed unhindered into his mind.

His heart was warmed as he realized how similar Belle and his mother were. Their smiles, their laughter, their loving spirits. Recalling that his mother had loved receiving bunches of flowers at the most unexpected times, Adam made the decision that Belle would love some flowers too.

"This is a mistake, you fool! You shouldn't –"

"Oh hush! I do not have to listen to you anymore. Belle's companionship has made me a stronger man, strong enough to make choices of my own. You can try your hardest, *Beast*, but I won't listen to you anymore."

"Do not be so rash in your decision to cast me off, boy. There will come a time when you will once again strongly depend on your rage to save your life."

"I highly doubt that."

After finding only a tiny handful of flowers, Adam returned indoors. He shook himself dry, similar to how a dog shakes himself after water has drenched his coat. The frigid days bothered Adam no longer; his body was now completely covered in thick hair, protecting him from the cold. Now the worst he ever felt was damp, which was a tolerable feeling compared to freezing cold.

The prince searched for Belle, eventually finding her in the ballroom. Adam lingered in the doorway for a moment so that he could observe the girl undetected. She sat pleasantly on the floor, smiling, and looking up at all the faces. Her lips moved as though she was actually talking to the statues themselves. Adam chuckled to himself; Belle would have truly been the favorite handmaiden among the rest of the servants, for she could truly make friends with anyone. Smiling, he walked to her.

"These . . . these are for you," Adam held out the flowers towards Belle. "They are a gift of gratitude for all the wonderful work you've done since arriving here at the castle. You are truly an excellent companion and servant."

"Thank you." Belle's eyes sparkled at the sight of such beautiful flowers, but she could not speak more than a whisper. Her heart felt glad to be appreciated, but Belle still did not enjoy being called a servant. She had just recently turned eighteen, and though she knew Adam did not care that such an honorable occasion had passed, Belle still thought that her age alone merited at least some respect from the creature. "They're beautiful," she continued. "I'm surprised you were able to find any this time of year."

"As you have seen so many times before, there are many enchantments in and around this old castle," Adam gazed off in the distance as he continued. "Perhaps blossoming life that thrives under the cold blanket of snow is one of them." Adam sighed, remembering how much his life had been altered by these enchantments. Curses, he called them. After sighing in contempt, Adam enquired of Belle, "Why are you in here talking to the statues?"

Belle shrugged, unsure how to answer the question. "When I left my home six months ago, planning for my adventure to last only a night, I brought with me one book. Since living here, I have read that book nearly a thousand times over.

"Surprisingly – I never thought I would say this – I have grown bored with that book; but I thrive on stories, whether I read them, they are told to me, or I make them up myself. So, I started coming in here every day to create stories in my mind, using your statues as characters. The faces are carved so perfectly, I feel as though I can detect emotion, personality, likes, and dislikes in just one glance. I know this all seems strange, but I really needed to tell myself some new stories."

"You love reading stories that much?"

Belle nodded. "And probably more. I have a hard time putting my love for books and stories in mere words."

"Then there may be something here that might interest you greatly. There is a room that may bring you some happiness, but I can't show it to you today; there are some things I must do first."

"I understand. I shall patiently await your surprise."

The next morning, Belle awoke to a strange and peculiar feeling. She knew she should feel refreshed, but her body ached so terribly that she considered never rising from her bed again. Even her spirit ached, which she did not know was possible. Her night had been filled with strange, almost horrible dreams; Belle had seen many things and people, but there was woman who stuck out to her more than others.

The woman wore a long, green robe that was intricately embroidered around the edges. Her hair was flaxen, her eyes were crystalline, and her skin was fair. After waking from her dreams, Belle could swear that she had seen miniscule diamonds woven through different strands of hair.

Every dream in which the woman appeared would end in the same way. Belle would watch as the woman bent towards her, kissed her cheek, and whispered words. Belle, no matter how many times she would experience the same dream, could never understand what the woman was saying. Then the woman would straighten up, blow a kiss with her hands, and then turn to run away. Belle would then feel herself rise up and walk around, only to find a green robe stained with blood.

The words "He will repent; you must forgive," would then echo through the air, slowly increasing in volume until Belle would wake with a start.

The only thing that drove Belle to get out of bed was the remembrance of the grand surprise that was promised to her the previous night. Putting a smile on her lips and love in her eyes, Belle left her room and met Adam in the castle's drawing room.

"Good morning, master."

Adam quickly turned around, caught off guard by Belle's sudden presence. Walking towards her slowly, he gently clasped her hand and said, "Please don't call me master anymore. 'Adam' will do just fine."

Hand in hand – which was a slightly frightening experience for Belle – Adam led her to the special room. Belle could not imagine a greater gift than what she had already been given; she was still shocked that Adam had actually told her not to refer to him as her master. Sensing that barriers were broken, Belle hesitantly asked, "Why the sudden change?"

"I don't know, really. But I . . . I spent a lot of time thinking last night as I was preparing this room for you. As I worked, I came to realize that I had never done anything for anyone in my entire life. I began to question my motives, and

I came to the decision that you, as person and not as a servant, were the reason why I have changed."

"I am honored to be considered the reason for your change, but I have done nothing."

"Nothing? Belle, you have shown me kindness when I least deserved anyone's affection. I owe the change of my heart to you."

Blushing deeply, Belle whispered, "I showed you kindness because that was the right thing to do. However, whether you realize this or not, only you could have made the decision for change. I cannot change you, Adam." Pausing for a quick moment, Belle continued, "May I be bold in speaking?"

"Yes, please. Say anything you like."

"I have seen the ways in which you have changed, but I ask for your forgiveness because I do not yet believe they are concrete adjustments. I knew a young man in my village who, for as long as I knew him, appeared to be loving and gentlemanly; but I have seen his wrath, just as I have seen yours. I respect you, because I have seen your heart change, but I do not yet trust you."

Adam nodded solemnly. "I completely understand. But, if I may be blunt as well, I hope what I am about to show you will help you find a way to trust me."

They stood at a simple door, one not as elegant as the door to the ballroom. Belle's heart pounded with anticipation and excitement; she had spent a long time thinking of possibilities of what the room could contain, but she would not know for sure until she stepped through the door. Rushing forward, Belle grasped the door handles and prepared to fling them open.

"Wait!" Adam grasped Belle's shoulder and kindly pulled her back. "If I may, I'd like this to be an authentic surprise." Belle complied and stepped back, laughing as she recalled the day her father gave her his little surprise. Thankful there was no blindfold; Belle only had to close her eyes. She silently gasped as Adam grasped her hand again and pulled her forward.

"You didn't have to close your eyes, but thank you for doing so."

"You said you wanted this to be real. I have found that lack of vision always adds to the suspense."

A few minutes later, Adam placed his giant paw-like hand on her shoulder and told her to stop. Belle smiled as she heard matches being struck, chairs being repositioned, curtains being flung open. *"I feel like a child on Christmas Day,"* Belle thought. *"But what's wrong about feeling childish? In this case, absolutely nothing!"*

"I'm done," Adam sighed. "You can open your eyes now."

"I . . . I can't believe this!"

As Belle opened her eyes, she saw the most beautiful sight she had ever seen. She, book-loving Belle, was standing in the center of the most extravagant, most expansive library she had ever seen. Case after case of books stretched out almost infinitely down long, beautiful hallways. Chairs, couches, and tables were everywhere, inviting anyone to come, sit, and lose themselves in a world of literature. Belle's heart beat harder in her chest, overwhelmed that such a place existed. "How . . ."

"My parents had this built when I was little; they had plans for where I was going to go academically. They planned for me to be a great scholar someday, perhaps even a famous author. But reading never held my interest, so these books have not been touched in close to ten years. Starting today, however, I want you to change that."

"You . . . you want me to read all these books?"

Adam laughed long and loud. "Well, I don't know if you can read them all, but they are yours. Read them whenever you like."

Smiling sheepishly, Belle asked, "May I read one now?"

"Go ahead, this place is yours to explore."

With a quick thank you, Belle was off, running free in a world that was meant for her.

Chapter Twenty-Three
He Loves Me, I Love Him Not

"So did these poor old lords, when it was too late, strive to outgo each other in mutual courtesies: while so deadly had been their rage and enmity in past times, that nothing but the fearful overthrow of their children (poor sacrifices to their quarrels and dissensions) could remove the rooted hates and jealousies of the noble families."

Belle closed the book gently and sighed. She had always loved reading aloud to herself, but hearing her voice softly echo around her in the vast library just added even more magic to the book. Gently pushing herself off the couch, Belle added Shakespeare's woeful, but romantic tome atop a large pile. Only two weeks had passed since Adam had presented the library to Belle, yet she had already read well over a dozen books.

"That was beautiful."

Belle let out a little scream and then apologized, blushing deeply. "I didn't know you were in here."

Adam's cheeks turned a crimson red as well, though his long hair and plethora of scars hid his embarrassment. "I was on my way to the garden, but had to pause when I heard your voice. I recognized a few of the lines from the book you read – *Romeo and Juliet*, I believe – and I had to come in and listen. My mother used to read that book as well."

"Well, I can read this to you again, but you have to tell me a story first."

"Anything," Adam promised as he lowered himself into a nearby chair. Before Belle came, he had grown accustomed to laying or sitting on the floor like an animal, but he had recently tried to become more refined. "What story would you like to hear? I must warn you that I am not the best of reader –"

"Oh no, the story I want to hear is not one of paper and ink but of words and memories. Tell me, what were your parents like? Were . . . were they creatures as well?"

The question stung Adam more than he would ever let Belle know. He had adapted to his present state of being so well, he would often forget how little he looked like a human. His heart sank as he realized that, because of his own hideous face, a stranger would just assume his parents were beasts as well.

Adam shed a tear as he said, "No. My parents were humans, just like you. My father was tall, with broad shoulders, dark hair, and a warm smile. My mother was beautiful, slender, and she loved to laugh. Both were firm in their teachings, but gentle in their affections for our family. They did not constantly have to restate their love for one another; their love was a bond that was well understood and one that could not be explained through mere words. My father would look at my mother and she at him, and you could tell by the light in their eyes that they truly loved one another."

"But if your parents were human, why are you –"

"A monster? I was cursed about six years ago to take on the appearance of a raging creature, but I was promised that, hopefully in a few years, a young woman of royalty would come to my castle to test me. If I can show her my heart has changed, then I can become human once more. That was who I was expecting when you first arrived."

"Oh. Well, again, I am sorry I am not the princess you were expecting to find."

"You don't have to apologize; I have really enjoyed your company." Adam tried to smile pleasantly, but his fangs were only exposed more. "And besides, because you have taught me to be kind, I feel like you have prepared me for the day when my princess redeemer does come. So, if we're finished with this discussion, could you read *Romeo and Juliet* once more?"

"Why don't you read to me?" Belle did not mind reading, but to hear that Adam now only thought of her as a "pre-test" was depressing. What she wanted was a friend, and she was eager to call Adam hers, but he still did not see her as such.

"Alright." Adam took the book from Belle's outstretched hand and opened the cover to the first page. He wanted to scream as he looked at the words; he was crushed to discover that he could no longer read. The letters and words looked like nothing more than illegible dots and smears on the paper. He laughed angrily as he remembered the last thing he had read was Enchantress' letter, the epistle of his doom. Embarrassed once again, Adam handed the book back to Belle. "I can't read this."

"Why ever not?"

"I have been a creature and an animal for so long, all that I learned academically has been removed from my memory. I can't remember how to read."

"I do not think anyone can ever really forget such a skill as reading," Belle said. Moving herself besides Adam, Belle opened the book again. "Try reading one word at a time, slowly, of course. I wouldn't be surprised if you could finish this book in an hour."

"I'll . . . I'll try, but I fear I might need some help." Adam cleared his throat and look again at the first word. "The?"

"Keep going," encouraged Belle.

"Two . . . chief . . . families . . . in Ver-Verona . . ."

And so, they read on well until the evening, wrapping themselves in the most tragic story of love that the world has ever known.

Winter soon melted into a beautiful spring, which all too quickly faded away into another summer and fall. Adam was now nearing his twenty-first birthday and he was heartbroken that Sabella Rose had not yet come to him. He had planned something special for her, but Adam was lost now that she had not come.

But one day, as he watched Belle dancing through the garden, Adam realized that she was something special. He found that he would be far better off loving a girl that was already there for him, rather than continually looking for a princess that was nowhere to be seen. He determined that he would give Belle a night to remember.

After learning how to read, Adam had slowly remembered how to write. The prince rushed to his bedroom, scouring every little drawer in each desk until he found a usable piece of paper. Writing quickly but as legibly as he could, Adam wrote a letter to an old family friend, the royal household's dressmaker.

The man had been let go shortly after the prince returned from his conquest because Adam knew a monster would never request new clothes. But now he was in need of a suit and he desperately wanted to give Belle the most gorgeous dress.

He signed the letter, and sent the epistle via a carrier pigeon that Adam found in the garden. Knowing that the dressmaker was proficient in his field, Adam was satisfied that he would be acquiring two of the most majestic garments imaginable. A month or two passed, and the anticipated parcel arrived. Adam struggled to keep the secret from Belle; for one, the young woman was more curious than normal women, and for another, Adam really wanted to tell Belle the surprise early. The prince waited, however, and his patience was rewardingly paid off.

"Belle, are you in there?"

Belle opened the door of her room and smiled when she saw Adam standing there, eyes sparkling; in his arms rested a package. "This is for you," he explained. "And if you would be willing, I would love to have the pleasure of escorting you to the ballroom for a dance."

"You want to dance? With me? Why?"

"Well, I know both of our birthdays are fast approaching, and I thought I should try and arrange something special."

"A dance is very special. I think I can get ready in an hour, if that is acceptable."

"That is a perfect time, my lady." Adam bowed low at the waist and turned to walk down the hallway, but he was stopped as Belle cried out, "Adam!"

"Yes?"

"Thank you. This means a lot to me."

Adam bowed again, this time in silence, and resumed his exit. Belle slowly closed the door; she waited until she could no longer hear any footsteps and then she rushed to open the package. She squealed unashamed, overjoyed at the thought of what might be in the parcel. When the paper was all torn away, a sparkling pile of silk and diamonds lay on Belle's bed.

Terrified of damaging the gift, Belle carefully spread out the dress. The material was the softest silk Belle had ever felt, and the design was more elegant than any dress she had ever seen. The silk was beautifully golden, sporadically studded with the tiniest of diamonds; tiny flowers made from lace that was the color of a blush sunset bordered the neck and hemline. Belle hurriedly tugged her old dress off and slipped comfortably into the new one. The dress hugged her sides elegantly, giving her the true appearance of a princess.

Belle lifted the skirt, which she found to be incredibly light, and walked to the nearest mirror. She twisted and twirled, inspecting every inch of her reflection. She sighed in awe of the beauty that the dress brought to her. But Belle was mortified as she realized how her hair was horribly upstaged by the dress.

Rushing to her satchel that she had kept with her since she left her home, Belle found her brush and a few scattered pins. She worked to get out every knot and tangle, satisfied only when soft waves of her auburn locks flowed around her shoulders. Using her pins, Belle pulled back some of her hair away from her face. She soon returned to the mirror, joyful to see that her hair looked simply elegant.

Then she just waited. Belle had committed herself to waiting an hour, but that was before she discovered how quickly she could actually get ready. She occupied her mind with books and poetry, trying not to think of how nervous she actually felt. Thousands of jittery feelings embodied her; she would feel chilled one moment and then unexplainably warm the next. She felt overjoyed that Adam had asked her to dance *and* had given her such a lovely dress, but her stomach tightened at the thought of his motives. "*Does he love me?*" Belle's mouth went dry at the question, and she felt faint as she tried to recognize her own feelings.

Belle paced about her room. "He took me away from my family, but he gave me a place to call my own. He treated me with cruelty, but he has grown to be almost caring. Do *I* love *him*?" Belle wracked her heart for an answer. "No, I don't! He killed fairies; his hands have been stained with blood. He called me a servant, treated me like a slave. He keeps me here only so he can practice being a gentleman for when his 'princess' arrives.

"I will go down to that ballroom tonight, but not as a maiden swooning in the arms of her prince. This is simply just a dance between . . . acquaintances. I love Adam as much as I love, oh I don't know, Caspar!"

The clock in her room mournfully chimed, telling Belle an hour had passed. Belle slipped on her shoes and quietly left her room. She knew where the ballroom was and could have easily ran there, but she took her time; Belle would have hated to give the appearance that she was eager to dance.

After another fifteen minutes or so of purposeful wandering, Belle found her way to the ballroom's entrance. Belle recalled the first time Adam had showed her that door, and she had to wonder if all his "changes of heart" had led up to this dance. Was he pretending to love her to fulfill an empty space in his own heart, fracturing hers in the process? Sighing, not knowing what to think, Belle took a deep breath and pushed open the door.

Chapter Twenty-Four
The Return

The ballroom looked nothing like before. The room was immaculately cleaned and beautifully polished. All of the statues were moved to the sides of the room, positioned like spectators about to witness a grand event. *"What a spectacle,"* Belle thought to herself. *"He went to so much trouble just to put on a show for a girl like me. I might as well match the façade."* Putting a cheery, elegant smile on her face, Belle glided down the staircase.

But all her doubts, hesitations, and grievances melted away as she saw Adam in the center of the room. He was also dressed like royalty, and he looked much more human. Adam, to prove his change, had worked hard on fixing his appearance; he could not remove his claws or fangs, he could not mend his skin or fix his hunched spine, but he was able to cut away some of the massive overgrowth of hair. His face was a little more visible, and that is what Belle noticed first. Though he still had many scars and long hair on his head, Belle smiled as she really saw his eyes for the first time.

"You came!"

Belle nodded. "You did give me an hour."

"Yes," Adam replied, "But I have been waiting for this night for many months now, and when you took a little more than an hour to come, I thought all my work was for nothing."

"Hard work never pays back with an empty hand." Belle found herself smiling again. *"Stop that,"* she scolded herself. *"You don't love him, remember?"* Belle's heart, however, was not really listening to what her mind had to say.

Adam held out his hand, which he had covered with expensive cloth gloves, and asked, "May I have this dance?"

Belle put her hand in his, but did not move. "There is no music."

Adam thought for a moment. "My father used to tell me stories of when he and my mother were younger. He said they would come down to this ballroom, and even when there was not a soul around to give them music, they still danced late into the night. My father would say that he and my mother would imagine a melody playing in their heads and that was enough for them."

Belle nodded and drew in a little closer to Adam. "Then that should be enough for us."

They danced for hours, neither one ever speaking a word. They just listened to the melodies in their heads and danced accordingly. At one point, Adam started humming his song; his melodies resonated within Belle. She took the time to really listen to what he was humming, and realized she had been singing the same song to herself. *"Must be part of the magic of this place."* Resting her head on Adam's chest, Belle made a wish. She wished that she could stay in this magic forever, never having to wake up to reality.

Suddenly, out of the silence, Adam asked, "What's the matter, Belle?"

"I don't know what you mean. I am perfectly happy."

Adam broke away and looked Belle in the eyes. "No, you're not. You have been next to me for the past few hours, yet never once did your eyes sparkle or shine like they do when you are truly happy. I thought all this would mean something special to you, but I can see by the look in your eyes that you desire something more."

Belle slowly nodded. "This has been wonderful, Adam; you've made this evening the most beautiful night I have had in an extremely long while. But standing here, I can't help but miss my family; I'd give anything to see them again."

Adam smiled as he walked towards the staircase. "Follow me; there is something in the West Wing that might be an answer to your problem."

"Please, no. I . . . I don't ever to wish to go back to that place ever again."

Adam nodded and promised he would return shortly. He ran off, hoping that what he was thinking of would actually help Belle. The prince quickly entered the West Wing, shocked by the realization of how deathly the room actually was. He looked around and noticed for the first time what an animal he had been; there were probably thousands of wings in that room, all displays of his bloody rage. Adam shook his head, remembering that he was up here only to get what Belle needed. Finding the shard, Adam rushed back to the ballroom.

"Here, take this. Speak aloud what you wish to see, and this will show you what you desire," Adam explained as he placed the piece of glass in Belle's hand.

"My father. I want to see my father."

The shard glowed bright and little emerald sparks flickered around Belle's palm. A faint image began to appear in the center of the mirror, growing with vividness until Belle thought she could reach out and grasp her father's hands. "Oh Papa," she cried.

The old man lay in bed, delirious with fever and guilt. Lilly sat beside him, rubbing her father's head with a damp cloth. *"They didn't listen,"* Belle heard her father cry. *"They didn't believe me!"*

"Papa, you need to calm down," Lilly cooed as tears illuminated her eyes. *"The more you rant the higher your temperature burns."*

"I let him take Belle. I should . . . I should have been a better father. I'd give anything to have Belle back here with us." The picture faded as Seymour fell into a horrible fit of coughs.

"They want me back! He did not mean to leave me here! Oh, he's so sick; he could be dying." Turning back to Adam, who already knew what she was going to ask, Belle requested that she could return home. Crestfallen and heartbroken, Adam agreed that Belle had to go home. He agreed to let her go if she would take the mirror with her, a keepsake by which to remember him.

"Belle," Adam interjected before she made her way through the door, "Know that I love you."

Belle nodded, smiled, and ran back to her room; she did not want to have to answer the question she was sure would follow. She could feel her love for Adam growing, but she was far from ready to admit any such thing.

Besides, her family was what was important now. Belle knew she had to get to her father, to tell him that she loved him and that she forgave him. She had to see Lilly again.

Saddling up Antoinette, Belle rode like mad, never looking back at the castle.

Belle rode through the forest into the early hours of the morning. She knew Antoinette was tired when the horse started tripping over her own hooves, but Belle couldn't afford to let her stop. She finally reached her home, a sight that drove her to tears. She pulled Antoinette to a complete stop when she reached the barrier of the woods.

Belle wanted just to rush in and fall into her family's arms, but she wasn't sure if that was wise. She had been gone for almost two years, and since she was almost nineteen and had lived through a trying time at the castle, Belle was sure that her appearance had changed and perhaps hardened since she last saw her loved ones. *"Will they recognize me?"*

Taking a shaky breath, Belle dismounted the horse. She walked cautiously towards her home, still unsure of how she would be received. But when a cry broke through the air, Belle began to weep unashamedly as she saw her sister run out of the house.

Both sisters ran towards each other, neither thinking of the impact of their impending collision. Lilly reached out for Belle and Belle drew Lilly close; there they stayed, their hearts healing in the embrace. Each burden the world had cast upon them and every strain they had felt over the last few years melted away. Their love for each other was whole again.

"I'm so sorry, Belle. We should have told you."

"I couldn't care less about where I came from, Lilly. All I want now is to be home with you and Papa."

"You mean you are staying?"

"Why wouldn't I?" Belle held Lilly out at arm's length, confusion covering her face.

"I always knew you'd come home, but I never thought you would truly stay." Lilly focused on the ground beneath her and lowered her voice to an almost inaudible tone. "What we did was horrible, Belle. I still can't see how you can be so eager to forgive us."

"Forgiveness will be a process that I will have to work through, Lilly, but you and Papa are my true family! There is a bond between us that is thicker than blood could ever be."

The sisters walked hand in hand back to their home. As Belle walked in the door, she greeted her father with, "Papa, I'm home." Everyone was moved to tears, resting for nearly an hour in each other's embrace. Belle gave her father the forgiveness he thought he never deserved, and Seymour gave Belle the love of a father she had missed so dearly. For once in two years, the Dubois were sure that their happily-ever-after had finally come.

Chapter Twenty-Five
A Devious Plot

As the winter months rolled back in, so did the crowds to Caspar's tavern; the cold always seemed to drive the men to the pub, where they could warm their hands by the fire and their stomachs with stout and ale. Caspar had loved winter as a child, for cold meant snow, and snow was fun. But now Caspar loved winter because winter brought more customers that brought more money to his pockets.

He had now become the richest man in the village, and that made him quite proud; and because he lodged with his uncle and had no family of his own, Caspar was free to spend the money he earned on himself. At the time, Caspar wanted nothing; he was, for what he thought he thought was the first time in his adulthood, happy with his life.

"Caspar!"

Caspar turned towards the crowd to see Louis worming his way through the masses. Their comradeship had strengthened over the past year, even though neither knew why. The truth was that both had been deceived by Enno and Anno, and they had become united under the common cause of deciding the perfect time to send Seymour away.

Louis had accepted the duty of watching the Dubois house; he was in charge of keeping note of Seymour's mental state and making sure the man did no harm to himself or others. Louis would occasionally report to Caspar, but the details were usually mundane; today, however, Caspar could tell that Louis had witnessed something extremely important.

"What is it, Louis? What has that old man done now?"

The young man finally was able to wriggle his way through the people and came right up to Caspar. Taking a moment to catch his breath, Louis leaned close to his cousin and tried to successfully whisper, "Belle . . . she's back!"

A roar of acclamation swept through the crowd as they heard that their quirkiest, but favorite maiden had returned to the village. Caspar was shocked to hear the news, but that did not stop him from beaming like a young child. He had almost forgotten about Belle, for he had become so consumed with his fame, wealth, and self-image. But just hearing the young woman's name, Caspar's heart leapt for joy then nearly stopped beating. "Where . . . where is she?"

"At her house! I rode out to check on Seymour again, and –"

Caspar was out of the tavern and down the road before Louis could finish his sentence. He thought he traveled to his love's house alone, but he did not know of the dark shadow that followed him. Enno was still certain that Caspar's life actions would reveal how they could use him to defeat the Beast. Enno did not know to whom Caspar was running, but the fairy knew that this girl, *Belle,* held a powerful place in Caspar's heart. *"S-s-s-she may be our leverage in turning Cas-s-s-spar's-s-s-s heart to utter hatred."*

Enno stayed back in the bushes as he watched while Caspar ran up to the door of a small cottage house. "How quaint," Enno whispered to himself. Disgust turned his mouth sour. He could not stand humans' satisfactions with things that were overly decorated.

But movement drew his attention away from the house and to the front door; a young maiden, who Enno assumed to be the girl Belle, opened the door and threw her arms around Caspar. Again, Enno was dissatisfied with humans. *"How can they be s-s-s-o comfortable with public dis-s-s-splays of emotion? Humans-s-s-s are dis-s-s-sgusting creatures-s-s-s."*

Enno observed Belle and Caspar, who talked for quite some time. Caspar eventually grasped Belle's hands and bent down on one knee, which Enno had heard was the human tradition for requesting marriage. The fairy smirked delightfully as he watched Belle retract her hand and pull Caspar to his feet; her face was pained and his was upset.

Transforming himself into a clear, completely invisible mass, Enno crept closer, knowing that this was a vital conversation. He settled on a step by the house, satisfied that neither one knew that a fairy sat so close, eavesdropping on their every word.

"You dare reject me again?!"

"Caspar, you are my friend, but I do not love you! Two years ago, I met someone who I thought was more of a monster than you, but I watched him change. You, however, come here and talk about nothing but yourself and your own personal gains. I loved the boy you once were: gallant, protective, and caring, but you have grown up to be conceited and selfish. I cannot marry a man like that."

"So you love this other someone?"

"I didn't say that –"

"But you do not love me and your heart obviously belongs to some man, so you must love this other man."

"Whether I do or do not should be none of your concern," Belle snapped, but then she sighed and her face took on a softer demeanor. "Caspar, we have not set eyes on one another in two years; why must we spend our first few moments together again in strife and bitterness?"

"Any strife and bitterness is thrust upon this conversation by you and you alone, Belle," Caspar stated with unnerving calmness. "I came here with loving intents and you shove me away like an unwanted disease." Caspar turned sharply and began to walk away. Before he was out of earshot, he yelled, "I don't yet know how to convince you, but you will be my wife Belle. There is no other pair more worthy of matrimony than you and I." Caspar continued towards the village and Belle returned indoors.

Enno knew where Caspar was going, but he now held quite an interest in this maiden, Belle. Moving as mist through the doorway, Enno spied on Belle and her actions. He followed her to her room, where he watched a much-undignified display of emotion; Belle sobbed for a long while on her bed before she reached under her pillow and pulled out a small, linen-wrapped parcel. Enno was fascinated by the piece of glass that Belle held in her hands.

"Show me . . . show me Adam!"

Enno breath caught in his throat as he watched the shard glow and slightly hum with life. But he could not believe his fortune as the forest creature himself appeared in the reflection. Enno stared at Belle's face, watching every emotion that crossed through her. *"S-s-s-she loves-s-s-s the Beas-s-s-st! How wonderful!"*

Enno flew back to the tavern, where he found Anno gorging down a plate of food. Anno had discovered a wonderful benefit to being invisible: you could never be blamed or hurt for the disappearance of someone else's food.

"Anno! Our plan is-s-s-s complete," Enno whispered.

The fairy recounted to his brother all that he had witnessed and heard. He concluded with, "Cas-s-s-spar loves-s-s-s Belle, but Belle loves-s-s-s the Beas-s-s-st. We convince Cas-s-s-s-spar to lock away Belle's-s-s-s father; this will convince the girl that he means-s-s-s to marry her and nothing will s-s-s-stop him.

"Belle will then do anything to pers-s-s-suade the people that her father is-s-s-s innocent and has a sound mind. If everything goes-s-s-s well, Belle will us-s-s-se her magic mirror to show the forres-s-s-st creature, which will frighten the people and enrage Cas-s-s-spar."

"Why will s-s-s-seeing the Beas-s-s-st enrage Cas-s-s-spar?"

"Because-s-s-se – and don't interrupt – Cas-s-s-spar is already teetering on the edge of ins-s-s-s-sane jealous-s-s-sy. He will s-s-s-see that Belle loves-s-s-s the creature and not him and he will do anything to rid any other love interes-s-s-st from Belle's-s-s-s life!"

The fairies went to work, rallying the people and whispering more lies that now was the time to rid the village of the quite incompetent, extremely insane Monsieur Dubois.

Chapter Twenty-Six
A Bitter Heart and Broken Soul

Belle awoke to the acrid smell of smoke wafting through her window. She expected to see roaring flames and hear cries of terror, but there were no flames, and the only cries she heard were of anger and disgust. Quickly grabbing her shawl and the piece of glass, Belle ran to wake her family; fear struck Belle's heart when she could find neither in their beds.

Instinct told Belle that Lilly and Seymour would be found outside, but terror tried to convince her to stay inside, away from danger. But Belle knew that if danger befell her family outdoors, then that was where she should go. *"I am not losing my family again!"*

Running outside, Belle found all the villagers gathered around her house, and most were brandishing torches and rope. Smoke filled the air, but Belle was slightly relieved that the fire was contained and not leaping onto their house.

She cried out as she saw her father surrounded by a group of men, who jeered and taunted him, rushing at him like hunters trapping a frightened animal. And *animal* was an extremely accurate term; Seymour cried and lashed out with hands and his eyes were wide with fear. Belle saw Lilly located at the outskirts of the mob, pleading for the people to stop and let her through.

"*Who has done this?*" Belle scanned the crowd, trying to look for anyone who seemed to be in control. Then she saw him, Caspar, leaning against a nearby tree. She caught his eye and he smugly leered at her through the shadows. Belle's anger boiled within her and she screamed in rage. "Everyone stop!" Surprisingly enough, the chaos was momentarily abated. Caspar slowly pushed himself off the tree and sauntered towards Belle. "What's the matter, Belle? You seem upset."

Everyone winced as a *crack* split through the air; Belle secretly hoped Caspar's face stung worse than her hand. "You know what's wrong, Caspar! Why do you treat my father like an animal?"

Rubbing his cheek, Caspar explained, "We tried to take your father along nicely, but he wouldn't cooperate, and then your sister tried to intervene. Before I could get a handle on the situation, things turned ugly and the mob had their way."

"First," Belle said, attempting not to sound as flustered as she felt, "Why and where are you trying to take my father? And second, you could have very well stopped all of this!

You started everything, and don't think for one minute that I am going to believe that you are an innocent being anymore."

Now Louis took his turn and piped up, "Your father has been raving for months about a wild creature; sounds like a thing that would come out of a fable. He's stark mad, he is! We all think, for his own safety and for the protection of the village, he should be put away, somewhere he can do no damage."

"Surely you can see, Belle," Caspar said coolly as he tried to wrap his arm around her, "That this is for the best."

"No, this isn't!" Belle shouted as she pushed Caspar far away from her. "Caspar, make this stop!"

"Marry me, and I will!"

Lilly and Seymour both screamed out in protest, thinking that Belle would finally agree. Belle, however, had no intention on accepting the offer, but instead pulled out the shard. "The creature *is* real. Show them Adam," Belle cried as she held out the shard towards the crowd. A picture of Adam slowly appeared in the glass's reflection. Everyone screamed when they saw the visage, terrified of the hideous, disfigured creature.

Belle ran into the crowd and showed the reflection to everyone who would look. "My father was never insane, he was telling you the truth. For two years I have lived with this creature, Adam, and I have had some interesting experiences. At first, he *was* just a monster, but now he has changed; he acts more like a human than any of you have here tonight. At first I thought him to be the most horrid creature in the entirety of the world, but now," Belle paused to glare at Caspar, "I see the worst monster is standing before us all."

Turning crimson from anger and the heat of the flames, Caspar shouted, "She's a witch! She has used magic to conjure up this image so as to frighten us all; she wishes to distract us so she can free her father!" Caspar also ran into the crowd, his words and thoughts guided by Enno's deceptive lies. "The entire family is mad and driven by magical thoughts and desires."

"What should we do, Caspar?" A burly voice shouted from deep within the gathering.

"Lock them in their own house until we return."

"Where are we going?" A stranger's voice cried out.

"We are going to hunt down this creature, this *Beast*, and bring back his bleeding corpse." The crowd roared in agreement and all the men ran to fetch their horses. Seymour and Lilly, weak with defeat, were pushed back into the house, but Belle stood her ground. "Caspar," she yelled, "Swear to me on the friendship that used to be ours that you will not harm Adam."

Before mounting his horse, Caspar walked towards Belle and cupped her chin with his hands. "I won't harm him, Belle, I'll do much more than that! I will kill him, slowly and in the most torturous way possible. I will sever his head and mount the creature's blasted face high upon my tavern's wall. Then I will make you look at it every day, every day until you finally realize that the fault of his death falls on you.

"I want your heart to break, just the way mine did, as you look at what remains of *your love* mounted on my wall; I want you to suffer until you realize that you could have prevented all of this just by saying 'yes.'"

Belle, worn weary by the night's events, fell to her knees and cried furiously. "What did Adam ever to do you to stir up such hate within your heart?"

Caspar had already turned his back towards Belle, but he shot one last glance as men dragged her towards her home. "He stole my love from me, Belle. I'd say that's the best reason to hate a man." Mounting his horse, Caspar rallied the men from the village with one shout and they all rode off into the forest. No one knew where they were riding to, but tiny voices told them where to go.

Enno and Anno sat undetected on Caspar's horse, reveling in their presumed victory. Everything was working out perfectly for them. They were extremely proud that they had turned and entire village into their own personal pawns. They swore to each other that the forest creature would be dead by sunrise, then they could safely traverse the rest of the woods, find the castle, and the at last they could end the life of the miserable prince! But after hours of riding around in the forest, the Beast had not been seen or heard.

"This-s-s may be wrong of me to s-s-s-say," Anno whispered into Enno's ear, "But what if the creature thirs-s-s-sts-s-s-s for the prince's-s-s-s life as-s-s-s well? What if he has-s-s already beaten us-s-s-s to the cas-s-s-stle?"

"That is-s-s-s actually a logical thought, my friend." Turning towards Caspar, Enno suggestively whispered the whereabouts of an old castle and explained that the creature may have taken up residence there.

"There's an abandoned castle not too far from here, men! I am sure we will find this creature there." Caspar shouted. And so the men continued to march and ride, not once complaining or asking why they were even out in the forest; each of their heads had been turned by Enno and Anno's lies that this monster was a danger to their entire village.

A few hours before dawn, the men discovered the castle; they were amazed that such a monstrosity had remained hidden from them for so many years. For a moment, quite a few men swelled with pride, knowing their names would be remembered for ages as the men who besieged the creature's castle.

"This is our time, men! We have a chance that few people get in there lifetime. We a chance to wage a battle, save our homes and families, and prove to everyone what kind of men we really are. I ask only one thing from all of you: leave the creature to me! You may lay waste to and plunder whatever you find in the castle, but I want to kill the creature personally."

Adam sat in the West Wing, watching the mob down below him. He knew they were coming for him, but he did not care to know why. He was sure that Enchantress had prophesied wrongly and that there was no Sabella Rose to come and rescue him. The crowd of humans were probably doing him a favor, ending his life and all; Adam could not imagine how hideous he would look once he started to really age. So, like a dog, Adam lay down on the floor and waited for death to find him.

The castle door shattered on the floor beneath him, but Adam did not even flinch. He waited, ever so patiently, fighting against every animal instinct that told him to run and hide or run and fight. But after quite a few minutes of waiting,

Adam decided he's give the hunters a little hint; raising only his head, Adam let out a loud, lonely roar. He knew he was successful when he heard the heavy clomp of boots run up the stairs and kick down the door.

A silhouette stood in the doorway with a long-barreled shotgun in his hands. Adam admired the man's muscular frame, satisfied that his destroyer was not a weak man. Though the light was dim, Adam could still see the rippling cascade of muscles that embodied the stranger. His face was chiseled and handsome, and Adam could not help but see the irony in the entire situation.

"How peculiar that my life, the life of a hideous monster, should be ended by one so handsome. Beauty always seems to be the victor; beauty will always defeat the Beast." The prince closed his eyes and accepted the end. After a few minutes of silence, Adam opened his eyes and saw that the figure still lingered in the doorway, probably reveling in his up-and-coming victory.

"So," the man spoke with a smooth, calm voice (Adam could hear, however, the undertones of anger), "You're the monster, the terrible Beast. You seem docile for one about to die; are you afraid to fight?"

"I *was* the Beast," Adam mumbled.

"Ah! You too profess your change. How noble! I've always disdained nobility; they always thought themselves better than the common man." The man struck a match, found and lit a nearby candle, and surveyed the room. "A relic room! You and I are the same in that sense." He moved around the room, examining everything he came across; Adam's eyes followed the man as he walked, wary that a stranger was muddling through his possessions.

Adam sighed and closed his eyes again. He had hoped the man would have fired the shotgun as soon as he had walked through the door, and Adam would have preferred that, rather than having the man inspect all of the room's belongings. Adam felt as though, just by looking around, the man was invasively exposing all of Adam's past sins.

Suddenly the man stopped; the flame of the candle flickered violently as his hands shook. In his hands, he clutched a helmet that was dented and tarnished. "Where did you get this?" His voice cracked as he lost whatever bravado he had.

Adam lifted his head to look at what the man carried; tears entered his eyes as soon as Adam recognized the helmet. The crest on the top identified the owner easily enough. "That," Adam began, "Belonged to my best general, Vicenti Liárd." Adam groaned as the scene moved away from ironic and fell into gut-wrenching pain as, on the night he was to die, his killer unknowingly reminded Adam of the sin that tortured him still.

"Why is the helmet not with your general?"

"Dead warriors rarely have need of their armor." Adam winced at the coldness in his speech; he knew the phrase sounded hard and cruel, but that was the not the intent of his heart. Softening his tone, he continued. "He died nearly six years ago. In battle."

The man lurched forward as if to collapse and fall, but he steadied himself on the ledge of a table. In a voice that was deeply pained and chilled, he asked, "How?"

Adam did not care to tell the story, but decided go ahead because he might as well tell one final story. "We had just conquered a village and . . . taken care of their queen in a way that should have shamed me. Nevertheless, I was hardened and called for the palace to be burned down with the queen inside. Vicenti was much more honorable than I, and he stated that the queen should be given a decent burial.

"But I was at such a horrible time in my life, I didn't care about goodness. I refused my general's request. 'Go fetch her yourself,' I taunted as I threw the first torch on the thatched roof. Vicenti tossed his helmet to the ground, his sign of resignation; he rushed through the doors, hoping to save the body." Adam hung his head in defeat. "He could not outrun the flames. I should have stopped him or at least gone after him myself.

"My men came back when the fire had succeeded, only to find Vicenti's helmet lying on the ground. They brought it back here when we all returned. That is why I have a helmet but no general."

All was silent for a long while, so quiet that Adam could swear he was alone in the room. Unexpectedly, the man screamed in terrible rage. "You let my brother die!" With an enraged growl, the man rushed towards Adam with such ferocity, Adam forgot about being docile and leapt instinctively out of harm's way.

"My parents and I waited for weeks, no! We waited months for my brother to return from you bloody war." Every few words, the crazed man would lash out at Adam with a long hunter's knife. The blade whipped wildly and rhythmically through the air, sometimes coming within mere inches of Adam's body. With each thrash of the blade, the stranger would scream again, emphasizing his anger. "You knew he was honorable, you said so yourself, and yet you let him die like he was nothing more than a dog."

Adam kept backing away, not willing to fight, but he also desired a more humane death and did not want to be butchered. He was about to suggest the use of the gun, but he was quite predictably interrupted. "And to think Belle loved you," the stranger scoffed. "Does she know what a murderous creature you are? I should drag her here and make her watch you die!"

The fairies were having too much fun for their own good. The exhilaration of the battle pumped through their veins. They were finally at the castle, which, for them, meant one of two things. Either the creature had already disposed of the prince – which would allow the fairies to kill the Beast for sport – or they would be given the opportunity to force the creature to lead them to the prince. Either way, someone died and that made Enno and Anno extremely happy. But they were shocked when they heard Adam's confession of Vicenti's death.

"That means-s-s-s,' Anno began.

"The prince and the creature are one!" Enno screamed, enraged by the story. Both he and Anno shrunk their forms and latched on the Caspar's shoulders. If they were visible, they would have appeared as two hideous shoulder devils, controlling their human puppet and smiling viciously. They shouted with Caspar and lashed out with the same speed as his knife. They continuously spewed curses, using Caspar as their mouthpiece.

"Kill him, kill him," yelled Anno.

Both fairies were so consumed with their rage that neither heard Caspar's comment about forcing Belle to witness Adam's death. They did, however, notice Adam's quick change from harmless to ferocious. Lunging at the man and grabbing him by the shoulders (by which he unknowingly pinned the fairies in place), Adam asked, "You would do that to Belle? You would put her through such a horrible situation?"

Caspar bellowed, "Of course I would! Belle broke me and in turn deserves to be broken herself; broken to the point of realizing that I am the only one who could truly love her."

"And you'd kill me just to prove your own twisted affections?"

"I'd kill many men so as to root out of any other interests in her life." Caspar drew his legs up to his chest, and with a powerful kick, he sent Adam sprawling to the ground. "And I'll kill you because monsters like you need to die." Caspar's boot slammed into Adam's ribs. "And I'll kill you because you killed my brother!"

"And we will kill you," shouted the fairies, "Becaus-s-s-se you s-s-s-slaughtered our queen!"

Chapter Twenty-Seven

An Unexpected Ending

Belle and Lilly sat in their bedroom, discontented with their current situation. Their father had resigned and gone back to bed. The girls, however, were furiously plotting their escape. All the villagers had returned back home, but Belle was certain that they posted guards to watch the house.

"We could try the back door by the kitchen," Lilly suggested.

"I'll try anything." Belle kept her voice calm, but inside of herself, she was a torrent of pain, anger, and heartache. She was incredibly upset that everyone was so quick to judge Adam and she was especially angry with Caspar. But Belle did not want Lilly to see just how angry she actually was; Belle knew she needed to be strong, knowing how frail Lilly's emotions could be. She even wondered if Lilly still loved Caspar.

"Certainly she has seen how cruel Caspar can be. I am the first to believe that anyone has a chance to receive redemption, but how long will we go on until we admit that Caspar has crossed that line?"

Surprisingly enough, no one was set to watch the back door. Both made their way to the barn, quickly found the appropriate tack, and soon began to saddle their horses. Not bothering to make eye contact with her sister, Belle whispered, "You don't have to come."

"I want to," Lilly replied. After a long pause and heavy sigh, Lilly quietly spoke, "I'm sorry you couldn't have a better birthday, Belle."

"Today's my birthday? *Hmph*. Of all the days to turn nineteen, mine has to be today." As she mounted Philippe, Belle said, "But this isn't your fault, Lilly; nothing has happened that you could have prevented."

They rode out slowly to the edge of the barn door, but they pushed the horses into a speeding gallop as soon as they were in the clear. Shouts of protests could be heard across the field, but still they kept riding. Belle took the lead once they reached the forest since she was the only one who knew the way. "We'll follow the river," she explained. "That's the quickest way to castle."

When they finally reached the castle gate, they were distraught at the sight before them. Men plundered the castle mercilessly, and Adam and Caspar could be seen brawling on the West Wing's balcony. Belle gracefully leapt off her horse and handed the reigns to Lilly. "Stay here," she commanded.

"But Belle –"

"No, Lilly. I cannot guarantee who is going to return out this castle alive tonight, so I do not want you to risk your life. Papa's going to need someone to look after him."

Just as before, Belle ran to the castle's entrance in the garden rather than going through the main door; trouble brewed everywhere, but Belle assumed that her safest route was through the garden. She passed by Timothy's statue once more, quickly wondering if the villagers would desecrate or demolish every statue in and around the castle. She hoped that by dawn everything would be set a right.

But as Belle climbed the stairs to the West Wing, she suddenly began to feel weak. She lightly swore as she identified the feeling; Belle had been having what she called her "wilting flower pains" more and more, but this had to be the worst of them all! Belle groaned as she felt her muscles slowly began to deteriorate, forcing her to drop to the floor. *"If I have to crawl to the West Wing, I will."* Setting her jaw and ignoring the pain, Belle managed to pull herself up. Through a series of sprints, stumbles, and crawls, Belle finally found her way to Adam.

Belle stopped halfway through the room. She saw Adam and Caspar more clearly now that she was so much closer. Tears fell down her face as she saw the anger that covered both their faces. She was so frustrated that, after all the peace she had tried to instill in both Caspar and Adam, the two men were fighting like animals. Belle was certain that Caspar had started the fight, but she was still slightly upset at Adam for falling back into his Beast-like ways. Belle knew she had to separate the two, but she could not get her legs to stand. So instead, she shouted out the only name that mattered to her at the moment. "Adam!"

Belle had attempted had to shout out her love's name, but her voice came out as no more than an audible whisper. Though she had not the strength to speak loudly, her voice was still enough to catch the attention of Adam and Caspar. The prince gave a long, burning stare towards Caspar before turning towards Belle. Arms outstretched, he began to walk towards her.

But neither Caspar nor the fairies were willing to give up the fight. Enno howled in a blood-curdling way, grabbed Caspar's forearm, and like a sadistic puppet master he guided Caspar's knife through Adam's chest twice and quickly withdrew. Caspar cried triumphantly as blood poured from the creature's wounds, but his victory was short lived.

As a reaction to the pain, Adam's right arm flailed; his mighty limb crashed into Caspar's torso, causing the man to double over in pain. When he tried to stand, Caspar lost his footing (Enno's and Anno's extra weight did not benefit him) and tripped backwards over a dislodged brick. Caspar crashed into the balcony's old rail, which gave way under the weight. Eyes bulging with fear and realization, Caspar plummeted to whatever awaited him below.

Belle dragged herself across the icy marble floor to where Adam lay. Pulling herself up right next to his chest, Belle stroked Adam's face. "No, no, no, no! Our tale can't end like this, Adam." Belle let head drop as the tears poured forth profusely. She could hear the faint whispers of struggling breaths, and she knew there was nothing she could do to save her love. Weeping and mourning, Belle laid herself on top of Adam.

After a short, gurgling cough, Adam replied, "I'm glad you came back, Belle. You were missed."

Rising back up, Belle repositioned herself so she could easily cradle Adam's face. "And I'm going to miss you if you leave me."

"Everyone has their time to leave this life, sweetest Belle. I am sorry for the monster I became. I am sorry for all the fairy lives I took. I reacted to my anger, and that was wrong. I also apologize for spending my time focusing on a girl to come instead of the gracious woman in front of me; I realize now that all I wanted was in you.

"I am . . . I am sorry that I could not have been more to you, Belle. Know that I love you dearly." Adam blindly groped for Belle's hand. "Your pulse weakens, too. Perhaps we leave together." Adam looked his love in the eyes one final time and then breathed his last.

Belle shook and sobbed, not understanding why everything was ending the way it was. She thought of Romeo and how he must have felt to find Juliet dead. "I'd rather leave with you now than live a hundred years without you on this earth." Belle looked over at the knife that lay on the ground, admiring the glinting blade; the edges were sharp and would end everything quickly. She imagined herself, dead and laying on top of her departed love. However, Belle knew she had not the strength to reach over a grab the weapon.

Slowly easing herself down, Belle lay with her arms on Adam's torso. As her vision began to blur and her heartbeat softened to the point of being unnoticed, Belle cried, "You're not a monster anymore, Adam, and I'll never remember you as such. I forgive you." Grief overwhelmed her as she spoke. Like a final petal of a dying rose falls to the ground, Belle's head dropped and all life left her.

Did you *really* think I would end the story there?

I just wanted to see if you were still interested. You may think me cruel, but a narrator is charged with keeping her readers attentive and the story exciting.

Let us continue.

Surprisingly, light was not the first thing that impacted Belle; she felt disembodied yet wholly new, which was what amazed her the most. Belle felt like she was in a tunnel, a meeting place hovering between two worlds. Though she could tell there was not much actually inside the tunnel, she could feel the hum of life in front of her. Glorious light beckoned her forward, but a faint longing her held her back. Belle sat down, unsure of where she was or what she was to do.

"Sabella!"

A tall, golden-robbed figure strode toward Belle with arms outdrawn. Her dark blond hair flowed behind her and her eyes sparkled with the grandest joy imaginable. The woman did not slow down as she approached, but instead wrapped her arms tightly around Belle, holding the young woman as if she were a little girl. "I love you so much."

Though she did not know why, Belle replied, "I love you, too." Belle buried her face into the woman's shoulder, breathing in deeply; she was calmed as she realized the lady's hair smelled of fresh air and dense forests. Her dress smelled very similar to extremely fine lavender, but so rich was the scent that Belle did not dare compare the aroma to regular lavender.

Pushing herself away at arms' length, Belle gazed at the woman with a mystified intensity; her eyes were strikingly blue and her face was smooth and white, showing no signs of age. "Who are you? I know you and yet you're nothing but a clouded memory to me, a piece of fog drifting through a dream."

The woman smiled and placed a slender hand upon Belle's cheek, sighing and smiling. "Such elegant words. I'm your mother, my dearest Sabella Rose."

Belle laughed and her entire body convulsed once. Then she too returned her mother's embrace. Both women held onto each other so tightly, intent on never losing one another again. They sunk to the floor, still in each other's arms. Belle, understandably overwhelmed with curiosity, begged for answers. "Where are we? How did you find me?"

"This is a critical, in-between place, Belle. Back there," Enchantress paused to point over Belle's shoulder,

"That's your life, uncertain of whether or not it is complete. Behind me is Heaven. You believed and have been given passage to be forever with our Father. This is a critical time because I believe neither you nor Adam have completed your work on earth and have asked that you be given the chance to return."

"Adam!" Belle gasped as she recalled the death of her love. "Where is he?"

"He's right over there, talking with his father."

"Oh. But you mentioned something about our story being unfinished. If the Father called us, should we not run to Him?"

"Yes, but this situation is slightly different. Caspar was tricked by devils to kill Adam and thus ended his life prematurely. We all feel that you have a calling to teach the importance of forgiveness, mercy, and compassion. Your story needs to be told to future generations. We want you to have the choice of whether or not to go back." Enchantress paused again so she could take a moment to look intently at her daughter. Placing her hand on Belle's shoulder, she sighed, "You have grown up so beautifully."

Belle smiled and took the compliment graciously. Though she knew in her heart what the answer was, Belle still asked the question. "Which mother are you? My real mother or Seymour's wife?"

"Your real mother, Belle."

"Will you miss me if I decide to leave and go back?"

"Do not hear my words wrong, but honestly, I wouldn't. Time moves so differently for us in this realm, I'll only have to blink before you're back with me again."

Belle glanced over her mother's shoulder to see Adam hugging his father. He turned and left down the tunnel. Belle looked her mother in the eyes, gave her a quick kiss on the cheek, and ran back towards her life.

Chapter Twenty-Eight
Change

Lightly falling drops of rain awakened Belle; the droplets were cold, but they did not quench the warmness that was within her. She opened her eyes like one who had slept for many nights and was just now ready to see the dawn. Adam stirred beneath her and Belle quickly pushed herself away. She let out a tiny scream, not expecting to see Adam's true self beneath her.

Belle's heart pounded and her breath caught in her throat as she noticed, for the first time, how handsome Adam was. Strong muscles carved out his arms and legs; his frame was slender, but sturdy. Waves of chestnut-blond hair framed Adam's strong jawline. Whatever scars had covered his face before had completely vanquished, leaving the prince's smooth and unaged skin visible to the eye of every beholder.

Belle cautiously crept closer. Deep in her heart, she knew the breathtakingly handsome man was indeed Adam, but she struggled to believe her heart. There was no conceivable way that he could be the hideously disfigured creature that she had known for years. *"If ever there was a man to be fallen in love with at first sight –"*

Belle did not finish her thought, for a cough and movement distracted her. Adam, arm gently wrapped over where he had been stabbed, moaned as he came to life. "Belle?" His voice was weak, but his tone was crisp and strong. Belle had heard the voices of mighty men, yet she knew of none who could match the humble authority that Adam's voice carried. Sliding up next to his still form, she whispered, "I'm here."

Adam did not hesitate in sitting himself up. He smiled and quickly pulled Belle towards him. Crying, Belle wrapped her arms around her love's neck as he enfolded her in his embrace. They sat there in silence, both taking a moment to appreciate the sweetness of life; there is a feeling none more sobering than the realization that you were dead, but were now alive again. "You look different," Belle spoke wistfully. She let her head rest gently on Adam's shoulder.

"So do you," Adam's voice was slowly drawn out and filled with unexplainable questioning. Belle pushed herself back and was surprised to find Adam's expression matched the curiousness in his voice.

"How can I be any different? *You're* the one who's transformed!"

"I hope you do not find fault in my assumptions, Belle, but," Adam paused for an uncomforting amount of time. His hand covered his mouth and his brow furrowed, and Belle could tell he was having an extremely difficult time choosing what words to say.

"But what?" Belle hoped her prompt would help Adam finish his statement.

"Belle, you look very much like a fairy."

Eyes wide and mouth agape, Belle took the glass shard from her satchel. Her hands shook as she held the mirror up to her face. Belle did see a slight difference, but what she saw did not lead her to believe she was fairy; her eyes were a little wider and sat on more of an angle, and her ears came to a slight point at their very tip.

She was about to put the shard away, but she felt a curious tingle between her two shoulders. Soon the tingle grew into a throb, which then changed into an almost audible hum; Belle's head dropped and she gasped for air. She could strongly feel all of her blood and strength rushing to her back. A light airiness soon covered her shoulders and Belle lifted her head, relieved that the pain was gone.

But when she saw Adam's eyes, Belle wondered what had actually happened. With gentle, trembling fingers, Belle reached over to touch her back. She laughed and cried at the same time as her fingers brushed against a soft, film-like substance that protruded from her back. Her fingers followed the edge of the membrane for as far as she could reach back; when her arm could reach no further, Belle picked up the piece of glass and handed the mirror to Adam. "Would you please stand behind me?"

Adam nodded silently, shock clearly glazing his face. When he was in position, he mumbled something, but Belle could not hear him. Belle took a slow deep breath and then cautiously turned her head around to glance over her shoulder.

Out of the corner of her eye, she caught her back's reflection. Between her shoulder blades flowed two rose-colored, intricately designed membranes. "Wings." Belle whistled in a low tone and her wings began to vibrate. They, the wings, were of the same hue as the most beautiful, blushing rose.

Turning around, Belle looked Adam directly in the eyes. "Looks as though you were right." Smiling, she leapt to her feet, a motion that felt lighter and easier than she could ever remember. Belle twirled and leapt, her laugh sounding like the dance of a thousand rivers. "Oh!" Belle cried and her hands flew up to her face. "I remember my name, well, my other name. My fairy name, that is. Sabella Rose. I am Sabella Rose!

"That was why we changed back to who we really are; I am apparently the one sent to examine your changed heart. I guess when I said, 'I forgive you,' I was unknowingly admitting you *had* changed, and that is why we are both the way we are now!" She stopped in front of Adam and crossed her arms over his neck. "Isn't this wonderful?"

Adam nodded, but his face was sullen. He smiled, though his eyes were weighed with a heavy burden. Gently grabbing her wrists, Adam removed himself from Belle's embrace. The prince took a moment to look Belle in the eyes, quietly laughed once, and turned away.

"What's wrong now?" Belle was so confused. She was ecstatic to have discovered her identity, but she was hurt to see how Adam had become. "Why can't you be happy for me?"

Adam stopped. "Because," he began, "As a young boy, I committed a crime against you. I don't think you could, or should, ever forgive me." Adam turned again to face Belle, ashamed for her to see his tears.

Every memory that had been purposefully locked away over the years came flooding in like a torrent into Belle's mind. The army, the prince, the forest, the hole, her mother. She looked at Adam; shock and unfathomable pain started gripping her tightly. Even though he was crest-fallen, Belle could still see Adam as he was six years ago.

Her blood boiled and rage stole her breath. She opened her mouth to curse him, but she stopped. Belle closed her eyes and remembered her mother; anger turned to grief as Belle's imagination took over and explained her mother's death. There was no doubt in Belle's mind that Adam had killed Enchantress, her only qualm was deciding *if* she could and should forgive him.

"*If he hadn't killed her, I wouldn't have had to grow up without a mother.*" This thought penetrated Belle's mind until her body shook with confusion and resentment. But then a heaven-sent peace befell her as she realized all the good that had come into her life. She had Seymour and Lilly, who had dutifully earned the title of family. She had made a friend with Monsieur Cartier, who had nurtured her love of books. Belle had grown to love Adam, which in all honesty, had been the most wonderful time of her life.

Out of all the good, the most important was that Belle had learned to be human; she had learned that life was a curious mixture of victories and trials, successes and mistakes. Belle remembered how many times she had failed over the years, and yet forgiveness was still given to her. Though her heart was heavy, Belle smiled as she looked at Adam. "I forgive you," she whispered.

Adam wiped away his tears and embraced his love, trying to be mindful of her wings. "I fail to see how I am deserving of you forgiveness once again."

"You aren't, but that doesn't matter, because forgiveness is a gift. Love, grace, mercy, and forgiveness: they are all gifts. Gifts to be given to those least deserving." Belle stood on her tip-toes and placed a gentle kiss on Adam's cheek. "Shall we go inside?" She asked, motioning to the balcony's door. Adam nodded, linked his arm in Belle's, and escorted her indoors.

"Your highnes-s-s-s?"

Both Adam and Belle turned around to see two lumpy figures kneeling on the ground. Their skin was gray and the wings that protruded from their bulging shoulders were stubby and dirty. Despite the creatures' ugly appearance, there was no mistaking them for anything else but fairies. Adam let a growl resonate in his throat; though they were older and grosser than when he had seen them, he still recognized them as the cowardly fairies that slaughtered his parents. "What right have you wolves to be here?"

Enno sneered at the prince. "Quiet, s-s-s-swine! We will deal with you later, but now we wis-s-s-sh to speak to our new queen!"

Belle's jaw hung slack and her mouth went dry. "Do you mean me?"

"Indeed we do, you highnes-s-s-s."

Though all her former memories had been restored to her, Belle could not ever recall being a fairy royal. "I do believe you have the wrong woman; my mother was a simple prophetess and nothing more. We lived in a little hut, far from the castle, which I doubt would be the dwelling of a queen."

Enno and Anno looked at each other, surprise clearly written on their faces. "May we s-s-s-stand?" Anno asked carefully. Belle nodded her head in silent response. Enno cleared his throat and quietly explained, "Your mother may never have revealed her s-s-s-standing to you, but you s-s-s-still have royalty in your veins-s-s-s.

"Enchatres-s-s-s was-s-s-s not in the line of either King Aso or Queen Jezé, she was-s-s-s the Queen of the Green Isles-s-s-s; though we would not normally acknowledge you as-s-s-s our queen, there is-s-s-s no other fairy with as-s-s-s much royalty in them as-s-s-s you" Pausing to bow low, Enno smoothly declared, "We are at you s-s-s-service, your highnes-s-s-s."

Belle held her head high, empowered by this new revolution. "I graciously accept your servitude. For pledging yourself to me, what may I do for you in turn?"

Anno smiled deviously and pointed a gnarled finger at Adam. "We want *him*! Our previous-s-s-s queen, Queen Jezé, commanded us to wipe out the line of the fairy prince, Prince Avanari. This-s-s-s *boy* is the las-s-s-st of Avanari's-s-s-s family! We ask that you hand him over to us-s-s-s, s-s-s-so that we may do away with his-s-s-s mis-s-s-serable life."

"*I have fairy blood,*" was Adam's first thought. He and Belle shared a quick glance and smile, and Adam knew she could see the anger in his eyes. Bending close to her ear, Adam whispered, "These fairies, *specifically* these fairies, killed my parents. I ask not for revenge, for I am putting that kind of lifestyle behind me, but maybe there is something you can do." Adam's eyes pleaded for Belle to act wisely.

Belle turned back to the fairies. Holding her head high, she asked, "I have heard your request, and before I render my judgment I must ask you two a question. As your queen, can whatever I say bind you forever?"

The fairies exchanged a slight glance of trepidation. "Of cours-s-s-e, your highnes-s-s-s," they slowly replied in unison.

"Then I command you to leave, to travel far away from here. You may never return and you may never attempt to take Adam's or any of his heirs' life. Now tell you me your names, first and last, so that I may make this proclamation ultimately binding."

"My name is Enno Grimmborne."

"And I am Anno Grimmborne."

"Then, brothers Grimm, hear my proclamation. I command you to go into the forest, make a dwelling for yourselves, and live out your days like the creatures you are."

"But, your highnes-s-s-s," Enno pleaded, "What about our race? How will the earth's progeny ever know about our special breed?"

"Make yourselves to be storytellers," Belle replied with an air of finality. "Weave your stories and leave them for the future generations." With a wave of her hand, Belle dismissed the fairies. A heavy gust of wind blew the two away, carrying them to a forest where they would live out the remainder of their lives.

Turning back to her love, Belle asked, "Shall we go inside now, *Prince* Adam?"

The prince bowed deeply and extended his arm to Belle, escorting her indoors.

Chapter Twenty-Nine
Second Chances

    Lilly sat on the banks of the river. Her face stung from the tears she cried, and her jaw trembled with grief and anger. She had been unintentionally forced to watch Caspar's fall; Lilly thought there would be no harsher feeling than that of watching the death of one's love. But she felt, in an almost tangible way, her heart shatter once more a few moments later.

    Though she had not seen anything, Lilly was certain of Belle's passing. She knew the bond between Belle and herself was strong enough that if one should vanquish, the other, not surprisingly, would feel a void almost instantly. Lilly had rent the sky with her wailing scream, sure that there was only darkness in her life.

    "Papa and I are alone once again," Lilly whispered to herself. The wind blew hard against her back, sending an uncomfortable chill to engulf her. Rocking herself and closing her eyes, Lilly hung her head in woeful silence. Only until she heard the scuffling of leaves did she look up.

    "Caspar!" Lilly rubbed her eyes, praying that Caspar was truly in front of her and not some cruel mirage.

But Caspar was indeed before her, appearing to be half the man he was. His face was penitent and somber, and he carried himself without an ounce of self-worth. Bloody scrapes and bruises covered his body, but the pain in his eyes seemed to hurt far worse. At the sight of Lilly, he dropped to his knees and bowed his head.

"Lilly Dubois, I have done you a great injustice, most likely worthy of death. I have been spared for reasons I do not understand. Perhaps I am still here, given a second chance only to beg your forgiveness. Though my mind has been cleared from an oppressing smog – I do believe now that there were evil forces controlling me – I take complete responsibility for my actions.

"I expect no grace or mercy from you or your family; I don't even know why God would give a man like me another chance at life. But I do know this: even if I were to die in the next moment, I would be satisfied to depart if I could only first hear you say that you'd forgive me. I've repented before the Father, now I repent to you." Caspar hung his head, letting silence fill the air.

He knew he should have been instantly killed when he fell into the frigid, shallow waters of the castle's right-branching river. But when he opened his eyes, Caspar began to feel like a newborn child, birthed into a brand new world. Unlike a child, though, Caspar knew he had no innocence; he remembered all that he had done, from scorning Belle to killing the creature. Caspar realized wrecking vengeance brought him no satisfaction, only guilt.

Lily remained quiet while Caspar had delivered his speech, honored by the man's repentance. Most of her heart readily wanted to forgive Caspar, but a tiny seed of bitterness warned her never to trust his words again. Lily knew she had always had a more somber outlook on life, but she also had the ability to see the best in others. As she looked at Caspar again, Lilly saw something genuine in his humble penitence. Promising herself that she would not be naïve if a relationship grew, Lilly said, "I forgive you, Caspar."

He did not weep, nor did he ecstatically cry out his thanks. Caspar simply whispered, "Thank you."

"You're welcome." Normally, that would have been all Lilly would say, but due to the surrounding circumstances, Lilly found she had the bravery to say more. "Let me say this, Caspar. I do, with all my heart, forgive you. Papa would always tell Belle and me that forgiveness is one of the freely given gifts in this world. Though the giver may have a difficult time in giving, the receiver has to do nothing to deserve forgiveness; that is why it is a gift.

"However, trust cannot be freely given. You have done some terrible, awful things, Caspar, and that is why I probably will not trust you completely for a long while." Lilly choked back tears as she realized how much she was sounding like Belle. "You claim you will change, and while I hear the same genuineness in your voice as on the day we first met, you will need to prove to me your change of heart and character." Lilly paused again, this time to let out a long, heavy sigh. "I have said all that I wish to say at the moment."

Caspar nodded, said another quick thank you, and turned to leave. Before he had walked more than three paces away, he turned and smiled at Lilly. "You're a very wise woman, Lilly Dubois. Perhaps I would be right to gain from this wisdom as life continues."

Belle and Adam heard the myriad of chattering voices echoing within the castle, and both agreed the voices sounded too pleasant to be a pillaging mob. Adam felt a tremor of excitement and forged ahead of Belle; on their way in, they had seen that the castle had changed dramatically. Adam hoped to find the last part of the transformation complete. Belle didn't know what to expect, so she lingered behind at the top of the staircase. Inside her heart, she knew that everything was all right and that she didn't really need to stay in behind, but an instinct told her that Adam needed to be the first to discover whoever was gathered downstairs.

"Sire," rang out a voice. Adam cried out with joy, ran down the stairs, and was soon engulfed by a large crowd of people. He ran straight to the caller, beaming like a little child. "Mr. Worthington, I'm so glad to see you again!"

Upon hearing Adam's exclamation, Belle gasped. Even though she was far away, she instantly recognized the man's name and face; he had been one of the statues in the grand ballroom! As she continued to survey the crowd, Belle realized that each and every person had been a statue that she, at one time or another, had encountered in the castle. "*Could flesh to stone have been a part of the enchantment that covered the castle?*" Belle pondered the thought as she watched Adam's interactions with the crowd.

"We were in the ballroom," another man interjected. Belle quickly identified the speaker as Jean Claude, the charming Frenchman, and she became enraptured by his rich accent as she listened to his account. "We were having a wonderful time celebrating the leave of Monsieur Worthington, when we heard a terrible crash and a rush of angry voices. We heard gruff, unruly characters rummaging through the castle. We charged out –"

"And quickly dispensed the miscreants," Mr. Worthington finished. He puffed out his chest like he was the only hero in the room; Belle wouldn't have been surprised if he would later go on to tell the story a different way, claiming that he had dealt with the crowd singlehandedly. Belle chuckled to herself and shook her head. Though she had not yet formally met the people, she could already tell that each had his or her own extremely unique personality and was quite special in their own way.

"Adam is fortunate to have such wonderful people around him." Belle rested her chin on her hands as she watched Adam going around and thanking the gentleman for their part in the dispersion, but she noticed that no one openly accepted his thanks. She realized that everyone was still fearful of Adam, for when he drew near, they would back away slightly and gaze only at the floor.

"Since they've been only statues," Belle spoke softly to herself, "They're minds have not yet moved forward with time; their aged bodies are in the present, yet they think they are still living in the past, in a time when Adam was still a vicious ruler. Repent, Adam! Show them you've changed."

Though Adam could not hear Belle's musings, he could still sense the trepidation in the room. Knowing what he needed to do, Adam knelt on the floor, hands outstretched to those around him. Belle smiled as a collective gasp, loud enough to drown out a small choir, filled the room. Tears filled everyone's eyes as Adam poured out his heartfelt apologies once more. He repented of everything that came to his heart and mind.

"We all know that I am a ruler worthy of no respect, but I hope that you will grant me your forgiveness. Even if you never forgive, trust, or respect me again, I will work my hardest to prove myself a changed man."

Mr. Worthington bent down and lifted Adam to his feet. "We know of the grief that has plagued you these last few years; hard times have even aged your face. But today, in the eyes and words of a man, I see a young boy we all knew and loved. I believe I speak for all of us when I say you have earned back our respect. Our trust will undoubtedly come soon enough."

"And we forgive you, too," cooed Mrs. Kettlery as she kissed Adam softly on the cheek.

Prince Adam wiped away tears and hugged the old woman gently. Addressing everyone, he promised that there was a terribly grand story he would have to tell. "But first," he began, "Let me introduce you to the fair maiden, Belle Dubois."

Belle, from the shadows of the upper staircase, slowly rose and then descended in a humble, yet regal fashion. The crowd parted like water before her, allowing her to enter and stand right next to Adam; everyone instantly noticed what a strikingly beautiful couple they were. The men chuckled and the women cooed, all knowing that a more fitting match could not have been made.

Before she had descended, Belle's wings had instinctively folded around her, which gave her the appearance of having nothing more than a sheer, intricately designed shawl draped over her shoulders. No one would ever guess her origins, but they certainly all sensed the specialness that surrounded her. Her presence sent chills down everyone's spine, and all immediately knew that Adam had found the right one.

"It is quite a pleasure to meet you all," Belle calmly stated. "I do feel, however, that I've known you for a long while. Adam has shared such wonderful stories about each and every one of you." Belle scanned the crowd and then looked to Mrs. Kettlery. "But where is Timothy?"

"In the garden, dearie," Mrs. Kettlery whispered as tears moistened her eyes. "That's his special hideaway place. He goes there often nowadays." Belle nodded her thanks and then turned to Adam. Placing a cool hand on his cheek, she said, "I would very much like to meet Timothy, but I have a feeling that you need to see him first."

Timothy sat on the ground, trying to find interest in his toy horses. They had been the last present Prince Adam had ever given him. The figurines were now as worn out and discarded as the boys' friendship. Timothy had once played with the little toys every day, but as Adam pushed Timothy away, the child began to hate the sight of the gifts; after less than a year of owning the priceless figurines, Timothy had asked his mother to store them away somewhere in the castle.

Recently, the boy had really begun to miss the horses because they had been the last connection between Adam and him. Timothy hoped that if he showed a renewed fascination with the figurines, the prince would begin to remember all the days they had played together; but even in Timothy's eight-year-old mind, he knew that was a childish dream.

"Hello, Timothy."

The boy turned around quickly and stared wide-eyed at Adam. His mouth went dry and his hands trembled at the memory of all the verbal abuses and near beatings Adam had given him over the past two years. Timothy noticed Adam looked older than normal, but he also knew grief and anger had the power to age a person however they saw fit. Curling his knees to his chest and wrapping his arms around his shins, Timothy quietly whispered, "I know you hate me, but please don't hurt me."

Pain-filled tears flooded Adam's eyes; the boy's words stung him in an unfathomable way. The prince had seen the fear in the adults' eyes, but the trepidation and heartache in little Timothy's whole demeanor hurt far worse. He crouched on the ground, unfortunately noticing the way Timothy flinched away from him. He knew mere words could not mend the gap between them, but Adam knew he would have to try and say something.

"I'm sorry, Timothy. I know I have become very mean, but I believe I can change my ways. This probably sounds like a terrible lie, but I promise I will make my actions back up my words. And please know that I have never and will never hate you, Timothy. When I yelled at you or called you mean names, that was because I was angry with myself, but I was too prideful to reprimand my heart, so I took out my anger on you and others. But you are my friend, and I will do everything I can to prove that to you."

Unexpectedly, Timothy leapt off the ground and onto Adam. His little arms tightly squeezed around the prince's neck, and Adam instantly felt the distance between them close shut. They were reunited again, like two brothers who had drifted apart for years. Adam could feel his neck dampened by Timothy's falling tears, so he hugged the boy tighter. "I forgive you," came Timothy's soft voice. "I've only wanted you to be my friend."

Adam pulled back slightly and looked at Timothy. "Then you shall forever find a friend in me."

Timothy smiled, but his eyes wandered away from Adam. Pointing to the window in the castle wall behind them, he asked, "Who's that girl?"

Adam didn't have to turn around to see who was by the window. "That is Belle Dubois, a very dear friend of mine."

"Are you two going to get married?"

Adam smiled, not really taken aback by the boy's bluntness. "I hope so, Timothy. I haven't asked her yet, because I need to talk with her father first. But if I gain his blessing and support, then, yes, I will definitely ask her to be my wife."

"Then you'll be forever friends!" Timothy beamed as he threw his arms around Adam's neck once more. Turning his head so that his lips were right against the prince's ear, Timothy said, "She's very lovely."

"Indeed she is, Timothy. Indeed she is."

Chapter Thirty
Epilogue

"You look radiant!"

Belle stood and smiled as Lilly entered the small room in the back of the village chapel. "So do you," she replied with much sincerity.

"But today is not *my* special day, so you look twice as beautiful."

"Yours will come soon enough. Papa has confided in me that he has truly seen a change in Caspar's character, but, because of his deep love for and desire to protect you, he is waiting to guarantee there are no relapses of any sort. We are all convinced of Caspar's love for you, but we all wish for you to remain safe and unharmed."

Lilly nodded and thanked Belle for her honesty. "You shouldn't be so consumed with my matrimony wishes, Belle, especially today. Enjoy your own wedding; you're only going to get one."

Belle smiled again, though she had not really stopped beaming all day. She had found the past year to be excruciating, since Seymour had asked for one whole year in which he could get to know Adam better. However, now that the long-awaited day had finally arrived, Belle's stomach had twisted into a series of fluttering knots; she was not anxious because she had regrets, she was eager because she didn't know at all what to expect in the years to come. But Belle knew, with their trust in the Father as their guide, Adam and she would have a wonderful marriage.

Belle had spent months designing her dress, and she knew now that every minute had been worthy of her time. Yet, as she stood, ready to go up and stand by her husband-to-be, Belle realized how all the materialistic details diminished in their importance. She believed that if she were to be wed in a barn with livestock as their witnesses, Belle would still be happy. She also noticed that, after a year of consuming her mind with every little detail, her only thought was, "Dear God, don't let me faint. Just help me to last through the ceremony."

The belles chimed and Belle told Lilly that was their cue. Lilly was to go first, then Belle, her arm linked in her father's, would make that long, beautiful journey towards togetherness. As they walked to their starting point, Lilly whispered, "You finally got your happily-ever-after ending."

"I don't think I can believe in being happy forever, Lilly, especially not after the past years' trials. But now I think I'll try to live each day to the best of my abilities, always trying to find at least one thing to make me smile. Granted, there will be tough days ahead; Adam has already mentioned the whisperings of a revolution to overthrow the remaining monarchs, but I believe the Father will help show us how each day is beautiful."

"It's time," Seymour murmured as his two girls approached him. Lilly kissed Belle's cheek and walked to the front of the chapel. After she had finished walking, Belle and Seymour followed suite. As they walked, closer and closer to the most handsome man Belle had ever seen, she thought of one other thing she would have to tell Lilly later.

"This is far from a happily-ever-after ending," Belle told herself. *"This is the beginning of a grand adventure."*

And what and adventure indeed!

So, overall, I know my tale was a little different from the fables you've heard in the past, but I will again assure you that mine is the truth.

What right have I, you may ask yourself, to retell the lore of old? I have the right because I am the only one that has the correct, first-hand account. Perhaps, I should at last introduce myself. My name is Jane Eloise, eldest granddaughter to King Adam and his queen, Belle.

I was always the only grandchild who showed interest in Grandpapa and Grandmama's stories (my siblings never had the patience to listen). Most children are put to bed by fantastical fables or other stories of the like, but I was fortunate enough to have grandparents that took the time to share of their youth. When I grew slightly older, I wrote their story down in this diary, for progeny's sake.

I suppose I should answer a few of the *whys*. Why is Belle never mentioned as being a fairy? The answer is rather simple; by the time most accounts of my grandparents' were written, Grandmama Belle was no longer a fairy. She had discovered that fairies lived much, much longer than humans, and she knew she wouldn't want to live a hundred years or so after Grandpapa Adam's potential passing. So, before they were wed, Belle learned how to trade away her fairy traits (just as Grandpapa Adam's own father had done); though she hated feeling like she had disowned her heritage, she knew life would not be as meaningful or worthwhile without her husband.

Why is Great-Aunt Lilly rarely mentioned? Some stories do write of Grandmama Belle having a sister, or in some cases, sisters. The belief that she had two sisters originated from town gossip; no one could believe that the beautiful, graceful, and, dare I say, outgoing wife of Caspar Liárd was Lilly Dubois. So instead of believing marriage had changed Lilly for the better, people surmised that Belle must have had another sister. The absence of Great-Aunt Lilly in most tales is also contributed by the fact that, since she was so shy most of her life, many people outside the village knew not of her existence.

That's all the questions I care to answer myself. If you still have questions, you may do one of two things. One, you can read this book again and concoct your own answers, or, two, research the history and find actual answers yourself.

I conclude my story with one final note. Grandpapa and Grandmama did live quite happily for the rest of their lives. I'm sure if they were still here, they would end their beautiful tale by wishing you many joy-filled adventures.

The End

Acknowledgements

Wow! I never thought I would have to write an Acknowledgements page, mainly because I never thought I would actually have a book to precede it. But the writing journey is complete and I definitely have some amazing people to thank!

First, to my parents. They were my biggest supporters and encouragers. Thanks, Dad, for being a fan of the book as well as its editor; who'd have thought that, back when you were checking my essays and papers through grade school, you'd be helping me edit my first novel? And thank you, Mom, for listening to my countless rambles as I was trying to figure out what I was even writing about. You were my priceless sounding board. Thank you both; your help and support are invaluable.

Victoria . . . girl, you've been there since the beginning. I still remember our late-night phone call where the idea for *Adam and Belle* was born. You've been the one to prompt my ideas and to help me through many writer's blocks. And thank you, *thank you*, for coming up with the name Lily; I think I wouldn't have been able to bring the character to life without such a fitting name.

Many thanks to my publishing mentor, Mr. Steve. You equipped me with such valuable information and gave me understanding on how to walk through the whole publishing process. Thank you so very much!

And to my English teacher, Mrs. McAndrew. You instilled in me a love for grammar and writing! I really don't believe this book could have been possible if not for your teaching expertise.

Thanks to my birth mom, Erin. I so enjoyed each and every conversation we had about *Adam and Belle*. I got excited to watch and hear you get excited about which part you were reading. Your input and encouragement really sparked my desire to hurry up and get this book done!

And finally, but nonetheless importantly, thank you to my family and friends (you know who you are). I wanted to call you all out by name and list all that you are to me . . . but I'd need another entire book to do that! So I offer up this minimal, but meaningful thank you! Each of you have helped me grow into who I am today, and for that, you deserve a countless amount of thanks.

Thank you everyone!!!